BALLROOM *Blitz*

LORELEI JAMES

Ballroom Blitz

Copyright © LJLA, LLC

Ridgeview Publishing

ISBN: 978-1-941869-32-1

*previous edition published by Samhain Publishing

The following story contains mature themes, strong language, and explicit sexual situations. It is intended for adult readers only.

Cover Design by: Meredith Blair – meredith@authorsangels.com

Cover Photo by: Scott Hoover

Model: Elvis Yadier

Interior Designed and Formatted by: BB eBooks Co., Ltd. – www.bbebooksthailand.com

Dedication

Thanks to Barb Hill-Kidd for sharing her insider knowledge about the world of competitive ballroom dancing with me. You got rhythm, darlin'.

One

"YOU CUT YOUR hair."

Jon White Feather pocketed the keys to his Land Cruiser and followed the sound of his niece's voice. She was sprawled on a concrete bench in an alcove between the driveway and the flower garden. He kissed the top of her head. "Raven, Raven, you been misbehavin'?"

"That is so lame, Uncle Jon. I'm not four anymore."

"True." He sat beside her. The last time he'd hung out with his niece, he realized she'd morphed into the too-cool-for-anything teen. As the fourth kid in a family of eight, she sometimes faded into the background.

It didn't help that Raven had entered that awkward stage, sporting acne, wearing braces on her teeth, glasses on her face and carrying baby fat. In the last year the normally outgoing kid had retreated into the world of books and video games. His brother and sister-in-law were concerned. Jon remembered Raven's older sisters had both gone through this gawky phase and now were pretty, confident young women. But Raven believed this *was* her final transformation and she'd always be the ugly duckling in a family of swans. And that broke his heart.

"So why did you cut your hair?" Raven persisted.

He shrugged. "I needed a change. Got tired of the braid. Needed something hipper." He exaggerated, tossing his mane like a supermodel. "So? Whatcha think? Is it rad?"

"No one says rad anymore, dork face." Raven brushed his hair back and inspected the ends that now touched his shoulders. "Actually, it looks good. Makes you look younger. Cooler."

Jon cocked an eyebrow at her. "Okay. What do you want? 'Cause you never give your old Uncle Jon compliments."

When she didn't answer, he patted her leg. "I was kidding." She finally raised her head and her soft brown eyes held such guilt Jon's heart sank. "Hey, little bird. What's really goin' on?"

"Don't get mad, but you're right. I do want something from you. But I didn't say that stuff about your hair to butter you up, because you really do look more like a rock star than you did with that old-man braid."

He didn't point out that her father wore a braid. Then again, his brother Jim *was* old. That made him smile. "What do you need? If it's money, I'll have to ask your folks first—"

"It's not money. It's…" Her finger swirled around the hole in her sweatpants. "I signed up for a dance class at the community center."

"Raven, that's great!" Her parents would be thrilled their daughter had taken an interest in something besides video games.

"But it's a couples' dance class."

"You want me there when you tell your parents about the boyfriend you're taking a dance class with?"

Raven rolled her eyes. "Do I *look* like the type of girl who'd have a boyfriend?"

"Not with that scowl." Jon kissed her nose. "Tell me how I can help you."

"I need you to take the class with me," she said in a rush.

He went still. Not what he'd been expecting. At all.

Before he could say no, she rattled off, "It's a three-week class, two hours a night, four nights a week. It's the really cool kind of dancing you see couples on TV doing, in those fancy dresses, all classy and romantic. I want to do it so bad, more than anything I've ever wanted in my entire life. I signed up before the class filled up, hoping I'd find someone to go with me before it started. And I haven't. I didn't tell anyone in my family because I thought they'd laugh at me." Her eyes were glossy with unshed tears. "You never laugh at me, Uncle Jon. You always tell me I can do anything I put my mind to. So please. I need you to be my partner."

Like he could deny her now. "Fine. Twist my arm. Make me say *uncle*."

Raven sighed. "You're such a dork."

"That's dancing dork to you, little bird. But I gotta warn you, kiddo. I am a shitty dancer. Like a scarily shitty dancer." When Raven opened her mouth to protest, he held up his hand. "I promise you, it's true. So I'll be your partner as long as you know it's at your own risk of broken toes."

"Same goes. Although I have been practicing some moves."

Jon watched as she popped off the bench and did some gyrating thing with her hips that he'd seen in strip clubs. Did all girls aspire to dance like that these days?

She held out her hands. "Come on. Let's go tell Mom and Dad."

"When does the class start?"

"Ah. Tonight. In an hour."

Shit. "Raven—"

"I would've asked you sooner, but you haven't come over. And we're not allowed to call you in case you're recording." She folded her arms over her chest, giving him an imperious look. "How long *have* you been home from your last tour?"

Two weeks. Two blissful weeks where he hadn't seen anyone. No one asking him questions. He'd slept in his own bed. Cooked in his own kitchen. Messed around in his studio until the wee hours. He'd needed to decompress after living on a tour bus for the last three months. So yeah, he'd avoided his brother and his large brood. Not because he didn't adore them, but he hadn't been the laidback, fun uncle they expected. He'd been a grumpy dick, so he'd stayed away for their own good.

"I know you're trying to come up with a plausible lie," Raven said with a sniff.

Jon grinned at his precocious niece. "I haven't been in hiding as long as you've been hiding your secret dance lessons from your parents."

Raven grinned back. "Busted. Now we hafta keep each other's secrets."

He draped his arm over her shoulder and they walked toward the house. "Please tell me I don't have to wear a damn leotard to this class."

She giggled. "A leopard-printed leotard. Like Tarzan. But you won't be able to pull it off with your short hair now. Maybe you can borrow a long-haired wig."

"Smart aleck. Seriously, what's the dress code?"

"The sheet said comfortable and casual. What you're wearing is fine. I'm gonna change."

Part of him wanted her to ditch the baggy clothes; part of him was glad for them because if she followed in her sisters' footsteps for the next teenage girl phase? She'd be wearing cleavage-baring shirts.

Once they were inside the house, a little person shouted, "Uncle Jon!"

Kids raced out of every corner, jumping like eager puppies. Six-year-old twins Jace and Hannah, ten-year-old Stephie and twelve-year-old Garth all talked a mile a minute.

The house was chaos central and the oldest three kids weren't home. "Where are Micah, Bebe and Cecily?"

"Micah is supervising at the youth forestry camp all summer. Cecily is lifeguarding at the community center pool." Garth peeled Jace off his back. "You'd know all this family stuff, Uncle Jon, if you ever called any of us."

"Ouch. You know that making me feel guilty ain't the way to change that, right?"

Garth snorted and threw a squealing Jace on the loveseat.

"What about Bebe? Doesn't she have her driver's license? I thought the two of you would be ripping it up, looking for trouble," he said to Raven.

"Bebe's working at Dairy Queen part-time and she's got a full-time boyfriend, so I never see her. Been a boring summer since I've been stuck babysitting."

"You babysitting for anyone besides the White Feather brat pack?"

"No." Raven stood off to the side, arms crossed, watching her siblings with the look of a put-upon older sister. "Dealing with them is enough."

"I smell food," Jon said.

When they reached the kitchen, Jon's sister-in-law, Cindy, exclaimed, "Jon White Feather. You chopped off all your hair!" She hugged him before she removed her oven mitts. "It looks great. Maybe you can convince your brother to do the same."

"I heard that." Jim rose from the table and hugged Jon. "Happy to see you, little bro." He held him at arm's length and studied him. "The hair does look good. But I ain't cutting off my war braids." He gave Jon a sly grin. "We've already got one good-lookin' rock star in the family. I'd hate to get a cool new hairdo and steal your thunder, eh?"

Jon laughed. "I missed you, old man."

"How long you back for?"

"Awhile. I'm burned out and need a serious break."

Jim's eyes went comically wide. "Wow. Never heard you say that before."

He shrugged. "Guess I'm finally ready to make some changes."

"I, for one, am happy about that. So can you stay for supper?" Cindy asked.

"That'd be great. But first Raven and I have something we want to talk about with both of you."

Jim and Cindy exchanged a look. "That sounds ominous."

"It is. Because I don't know any other way to break it to you."

"What?"

Jon hung his head. "Raven and I have been infected with boogie fever. And the only cure is to put on our dancin' shoes and head on down to funky town."

Two

MAGGIE BUCHANAN LOOKED around the community center gym. No barre or mirrors, but the large wooden floor was excellent for movement and would accommodate all the couples that had signed up for class. By the time she'd finished warming up, her mentor, friend and official dance partner, Seth Fordham, wandered in, looking fantastic, as usual. Seth was a handsome, well-built man and his charm was evident, especially on the dance floor.

Seth grinned. "You ready for this?"

"I guess."

"What's the plan?"

It was weird for her instructor to ask her for direction. "I figured we'd stick to the basics. Jitterbug. The waltzes. Tango. Foxtrot. Two-step. Polka. Schottische. Line dancing."

"Sounds good. With the exception of spending too much time on the schottische. No one ever gets that. We should touch on it, as far as form and technique, but move on to something else."

"What do you suggest?"

"Extend the jitterbug class another night since it's so popular. And…" Seth wore an amused expression. "Add a hip-hop class."

Maggie shook her head. "No hip hop."

"Why not?"

Because I'll look like an idiot hopping around, trying to be hip. "Because I'm not comfortable teaching a dance style I'm not familiar with."

"Which is exactly why you should do it. Dance is dance, Maggie." Seth bumped her with his hip. "Come on. It'll be good for you."

"Can you really see me popping and locking?"

"We'll see, won't we?" Seth scrolled through his MP3 player and plugged it into the sound system. Then he faced her. "Assume the position."

"You're serious."

"Completely. I know you're a fast learner." He performed some side-to-side movement with his upper body that looked like a funky robot while his bottom half slid the opposite direction.

"Where did you learn that?"

"Gay dance clubs."

Maggie groaned. "Unfair advantage."

"When we compete in a big city, I'll let you be my fag hag and we can hit the clubs. The way we dance together will blow their minds."

"Show off."

"So we'll work on some hip-hop moves to loosen you up at rehearsal tonight."

Part of the reason Seth had agreed to help her teach this class was to rehearse afterward. Their first competition was coming up in a little over a month. "All right. I'll set up the registration table."

As Maggie tracked down pens and nametags, she thought about how much her life had changed in the last six months.

She hated the term *corporate downsizing*, but it'd happened to her. After college graduation, she'd spent five years traveling the U.S. as a troubleshooter at a top Midwest computer security company. When the company was parted out, she was transferred to a smaller division at an Air Force base in South Dakota, where she'd spent the last four years.

Then six months ago…poof. Unemployed. At age thirty-two.

The economy sucked and full-time jobs were scarce in her field. Maggie probably could've found something if she'd been willing to relocate, but her grandmother had died suddenly and her brother and sister-in-law were having their first baby. Since Grandma Ingrid had left Maggie the small family cabin outside Spearfish, she'd sold her condo in Rapid City and moseyed up the road fifty miles to be closer to her family.

She'd found a half-time position at a doctor's office, computerizing decades' worth of medical records. She was overqualified, but the position offered health benefits and she didn't mind being jammed in a small cubicle. She'd also picked up a part-time gig teaching computer literacy in the afternoons at the library, both community centers and the senior center.

Without the grind of a fifty-hour workweek and very low living expenses, Maggie had time to reflect on her life. What she'd accomplished. What she was missing. What would make her life better.

And that answer had been a no-brainer.

Dancing.

She'd missed dancing. The physical exertion; the stretch and pull of her muscles. The pure exhilaration of performing; the rush when she and her partner were in perfect synch.

Until she'd lost her job, Maggie hadn't realized how much of herself she'd left behind when she'd given up competitive ballroom dancing in college to focus on finishing her degree.

She'd understood her brother Billy's logic—career first, hobby second. But what he'd never understood; dancing hadn't ever been "just" a hobby to her during her formative years. She'd lived it, breathed it, dreamed it. While other girls had posters of teen heartthrob stars on their walls growing up, Maggie had pictures of Baryshnikov. Martha Graham. Fred Astaire and Ginger Rogers.

During the summer before her senior year of high school, her father had died, leaving Maggie with her crazy, grief-stricken mother. Dance became her refuge. She'd been proficient enough to earn a dance scholarship to a small private college in New York City. But after a year of living with her sister Lacy and seeing firsthand all the dancers waiting tables while awaiting their big break, she fled the big city and the cynicism.

So Maggie had returned to her home state, enrolled in a technology program at the local university. But a funny thing happened sophomore year on the way to her statistics class— she accidentally wandered into the fine arts building and a competitive ballroom dancing class.

Over the years Maggie had watched the major competitions on TV, sighing over the beautiful costumes, the glamor and grace of the couples. So it'd shocked her when the instructor chewed her out for being late, demanding she get in line for a partner.

Rather than calling more attention to herself, she'd obeyed.

In retrospect, wandering into the wrong building had been the best mistake she'd ever made. Turned out, the years she'd spent learning ballet, tap, jazz and modern gave her a great foundation for ballroom dancing. The teacher had been so impressed that he'd introduced her to Booker White, the owner of the biggest dance studio in the area.

Maggie hadn't told her family about her newfound passion. While she and her partner Miles racked up wins and were the top couple at the Booker White Dance Studio, her grades suffered. Although the studio paid for costumes, training, entry fees and hotels, she was responsible for paying her other travel expenses. And in those two years, she spent part of her funds allocated for extra college expenses on dance competitions.

That's when Billy had intervened. He'd convinced her that an activity she had to keep from her family wasn't healthy; she'd dropped out of dance, focused on school and hadn't looked back.

Until now.

Her grin was pure joy as members of the class started to trickle in, their excitement warring with nervousness—exactly the same way she felt.

Seth greeted them at the door before directing them to Maggie. The class signup sheet had been filled weeks ago and the mix of couples was more eclectic than she'd imagined.

After checking in newlyweds and married couples of all ages, Maggie looked up to the next couple in line.

Holy cow.

The Native American man standing before her was breathtaking on a purely physical level. Shoulder-length black hair. Sharply defined facial features. His brilliant white smile set off his golden coloring to perfection. And his eyes. A stunning shade of blue. He wore a sleeveless T-shirt that revealed ripped biceps, triceps and forearms. When she met his gaze, he seemed amused by her blatant once-over and she blushed deeply.

The young girl with him, however, wasn't amused. "I'm Raven White Feather."

Maggie's gaze winged between them. Father and daughter? Although this beautiful man looked a little young to have a teenager. Feeling unnerved by her immediate and unexpected attraction to the man, she was happy to refocus on the girl. "Welcome, Raven." She checked her name off the list, but noticed her companion's name had been left blank. "And who will you be partnered with?"

"This is my uncle."

The man offered his hand and a smile. "Jon White Feather."

"I'm Maggie Buchanan."

"Buchanan?" he repeated, retaining hold of her hand longer than polite. "Any relation to Eden?"

"Yes. She's married to my brother, Billy. How do you know Eden?"

"Eden and I palled around for a few years. I forget Spearfish is such a small town. I'm surprised we haven't crossed paths before now since your brother Billy and my brother Jim are partners in Feather Light. This is Jim's daughter."

She smiled at Raven, touched by the way she leaned back when her uncle squeezed her shoulders. "You guys go ahead and fill out your nametags."

A rancher and his wife from Sundance were the last couple to arrive.

Seth looked up from fiddling with the sound system. "You spent extra time with those two students. Any problems?"

"No. They know my brother and sister-in-law. Everyone on the list is here."

"Let's get started."

She stepped in front of the group. "Good evening, everyone. Welcome to Couples Dancing 101. My name is Maggie Buchanan and I'll be one of your instructors for this three-week session.

"Why am I qualified to teach dance classes? Not only did I dance ballet, tap, jazz and modern during my formative years, I danced competitively in college in the American style of ballroom dancing. What does that mean?" She paused. "Lots of blisters and calluses from hours upon hours of practice."

Muted laughter encouraged her to continue.

"That's not what we're expecting out of you, but we will be

teaching several different dances."

Jon raised his hand before she could ask for questions.

It figured. "Yes?"

"Can you explain what you mean by competitive ballroom dancing?"

"To be a competitor in the American rhythm style, a professional dancer is paired with an amateur and that couple is judged on five different dances. The professional, such as Seth here, must be employed full-time as a dance instructor. Someone like me, while having a dance background, is considered the amateur because dancing or teaching dance isn't my main source of income. But it is a source of joy." Maybe that'd been too corny. Her cheeks heated and she broke eye contact with the captivating Jon White Feather.

Seth took the floor. "I'm Seth Fordham and like Maggie said, I'm a professional dancer. I moved home to South Dakota last year and I run a dance studio in Rapid City. My background is in theatrical dance. I've performed with traveling musical productions in the U.S. and abroad, as well as living every dancer's dream of performing on Broadway. My career was cut short by a freak accident and after two years of rehab, I decided to share my love of dance by teaching." Seth hip-checked Maggie. "And I've finally convinced my lovely Maggie here to jump back into the world of competitive dance as my partner."

Again, Maggie felt Jon's eyes on her. In fact, he'd kept his focus on her the entire time Seth had been speaking, but she hadn't dared look his way—difficult as that'd been—because the man defined distraction of the best kind.

"Any more questions?" Seth asked.

No one spoke up.

"Good. Then let's get started," Maggie said. "Tonight we'll begin with the basic jitterbug. Seth and I will first demonstrate the dance at a normal speed. Then we'll slow it down and break it down, step by step. So gather in a circle. This first part is easy because all you have to do is watch."

Seth turned on the music. He took Maggie's hand and they automatically walked together as if they'd stepped onto the competition floor. Seth had chosen "In the Mood" and they stuck to basic steps, adding in a few turns, but no double hops, double cuts or double twists.

When the song and dance ended, applause rang out.

Seth spun her into a curtsey and he took a bow.

"Now we'll break it down. First thing you'll notice is how we hold our hands."

After the demonstration, the female newlywed asked, "Does it matter who's leading in how you hold hands?"

"For the sake of simplicity," Seth said, "let's assume the men are in the lead. So guys, hold your hands like this."

Grumbling from the women.

"Ladies," Maggie interjected, "I'm an equal rights supporter, but in this case, Seth is in charge of showing the male steps, and I'm tasked with teaching the female partner steps because it'll be easier. And remember, just because a man has the lead on the dance floor, doesn't grant him the right to retain control off the dance floor."

Several women laughed and nudged their partners.

Maggie's gaze snagged Jon's. Everything about him said *man in charge, all the time.* Normally men like that didn't appeal to her, but seeing him so sweet and funny with his niece intrigued her—beyond the fact he was such a gorgeous male specimen.

She and Seth went through the steps slowly, then had the students perform the steps with them and finally on their own. They wandered through the group. If a couple was struggling, Maggie would dance with the man while the woman watched, then Seth would dance with the woman while the man watched. Usually when the couple was put back together, their technique had improved.

When they reached Raven and Jon, she heard them arguing in low tones. "You two do not look like you're having fun. Anything we can help with?"

Raven pointed at her uncle. "Yes. He keeps doing it wrong. He steps too close and then too far back."

"Someone wasn't paying attention when the instructors

said the men were supposed to lead," Jon said tersely.

Seth intervened. "Show us the problem."

Jon held out his hands and Raven snatched them. The first few movements were decent, but then Jon completely lost the rhythm.

"Hold on a second. Watch us." Seth took Maggie's hands. "See what we're doing with our arms and our feet?" She and Seth demonstrated. "Keep it smooth and tight."

Jon had crossed his arms over his chest. He didn't look belligerent, just frustrated. "Isn't that what I was doing?"

Maggie, Raven and Seth all said, "No."

When Seth danced with Raven, she followed his lead without issue.

Jon sighed and lightly nudged his niece. "Looks like I'm the one with two left feet, eh? You sure you want me for your dance partner, Raven?"

His amused resignation had Maggie stepping forward to reassure him. "Let's see if I can help." She took Jon's hands and they were face to face. And what a face it was.

Jon stared at her, as if he liked what he saw, and tightened his grip when she attempted to retreat. "Is this too close?" he murmured.

"For dancing? Yes."

He flashed an unrepentant grin. "Guess I wasn't thinking about dancing."

Me either. "So, Mr. White Feather—"

"Jon. If I'm gonna be stomping on your feet, call me Jon."

Such a charmer. "Okay, Jon. Start with your right foot. Step. Together. Good. Now, step back. No. Stop. You don't have to alternate feet."

He froze. "I don't?"

"No." When their eyes met, her belly dipped. "Now, try it with Raven."

She turned and addressed the class, grateful for a diversion from the engaging man. "Let's add faster music."

She and Seth wandered through the couples separately. Most had mastered the basic steps. When Maggie glanced over to see Jon and Raven's progress, she half expected that once the music began their rhythm issues would work out. But music had made it worse.

Raven looked ready to cry. Jon looked defeated. Not good.

Seth caught her eye and they headed back to help.

"Heya, teach, back so soon?" Jon said nonchalantly. "I thought I had the hang of it until that pesky music screwed me up."

"Have you tried counting to keep the beat? One, two, three, four?" Seth asked.

"Of course."

"Let's see how you're keeping time." Maggie clasped Jon's hands, feeling that magnetic pull again. "Bring your partner toward you on every other beat. Like this."

Jon tried it, but he kept coming in a beat late, on the third beat, instead of the second. Every time.

She bit back a groan. He might be a fascinating combination of self-deprecating and charming, but the man could not keep time.

Raven threw up her hands. "See? I told you. It's not me, Uncle Jon. It's you."

"I'll remind you, darlin' niece, you roped me into this class. And I warned you I was sadly lacking in dancing skills," he said tightly.

"But dancing is about rhythm. That should be easy for you. Don't you count when you're playing?"

"Yeah, but it's not the same. I don't think about it. I just do it."

"Excuse me," Seth said. "Playing what?"

"The drums."

Maggie's jaw dropped. "*You* play the drums?"

"Yep." Jon's eyes narrowed. "Why are you so shocked?"

"Because you have absolutely no sense of rhythm."

Jon threw back his head and laughed. "Doll face, you are the first woman who's ever said that to me."

Three

MAGGIE BLUSHED.

Raven said, "Eww, Uncle Jon!"

Seth smirked. But he rallied to Jon's defense. "Regardless, Mr. White Feather, it's obvious you don't have rhythm when it comes to *dancing*. So for now, it's best if I work with Raven."

Bonus. That'd pair him with the very sexy Maggie Buchanan for the remainder of class and Jon was all over that.

"…and you will watch us and learn."

Jon's gaze snapped to Seth. "Excuse me? That sounded like I've been benched."

"Only briefly. For tonight."

He looked at Maggie, but she'd floated off to help another couple.

So Jon had to stand there, propped against the wall like some second stringer. Studying another guy's feet, arms, hips and ass moving was fucked up on several levels. He'd never get this formal dancing shit, which was why he'd always limited his dancing to the slow type or the mattress type.

His focus strayed to Maggie, performing some cha-cha move that shook her ass enticingly. Way too enticingly; his brain conjured images of them doing a little mattress dancing, her perfect butt in his hands, his pelvis doing a slow bump and grind into hers as he tasted that pretty pink mouth.

A throat clearing caught his attention and Seth looked at him pointedly.

Jon shot him a sheepish grin. But he did manage to pay attention for the remainder of class. Raven was getting a lot out of the one-on-one instruction, including heaps of praise from Seth. And his niece's beaming face reminded Jon why he was here in the first place.

Raven was so anxious to leave after class finished that he couldn't shake the niggling feeling he'd somehow embarrassed her. He hoped the second night would go better than the first.

BUT THE SECOND night was more of the same torture. Jon was hapless and Raven tried not to act annoyed or mortified about the extra attention they received from the instructors because of his screw ups.

However, Jon certainly didn't mind having Maggie's soft curves pressed against him as she walked him through the dance steps. The woman was an enigma; confidently giving instructions to the entire class and yet blushing so prettily when they were pressed body to body. He was actually sorry when class ended.

After the rest of the students took off, Jon noticed Raven wasn't racing out the door, but in deep conversation with Seth. He wandered over to where Maggie sat on the bench, changing shoes.

"So it is true," he said, sitting sideways on the bleachers beside her.

Maggie glanced up. "What is true?"

"There is such a thing as putting on your dancing shoes."

Lame, Jon.

"Different types of dancing shoes for different dances. Probably like you use different drums for different parts of a song?"

"You'd be correct." He angled forward. "So while I've got you alone…give it to me straight. Am I failing class?"

The corners of her lips curled into a smile even as she remained focused on buckling her shoe. "This isn't a pass-fail situation. I'm giving you an A for extra effort." Maggie's eyes met his briefly before her attention drifted to his arms. Her gaze started at his wrist and moved up to his bicep. "I'll admit I've been admiring your cool tattoos during class."

"Do you have any tats?"

"No. Never had much chance to see artwork designs up

close to see what my options are."

He held his arms out. "Go ahead and take a closer look if you want. See if there's anything you like." *Feel free to touch as much as you want.*

Her eyes clearly broadcast *I want*, even if her alluring mouth stayed closed.

The first tentative touch on his forearm was potent as an electric charge. He held himself still, willing that charge not to travel straight to his dick.

Her cheeks were flushed. Her blue eyes bright. Tendrils of reddish-blond hair had escaped from her tight bun, tempting Jon to loosen it completely and crush the soft strands in his hands. Or smooth the strands back into place just to touch that creamy-looking skin. Maggie unsettled him. She was wholesome looking and a little shy—not his usual type. So his immediate attraction to her was baffling. Not unwelcome, just confusing. Question was, did she feel the same pull?

Yes, if he went by the way her hand trembled when she touched him.

When her soft fingertip drifted over the crease of his arm, he bit back a growl. Oblivious to his response, she continued the northerly progression, one hand clamped around his wrist, the other hand driving him out of his mind with a mix of innocent curiosity and overt sensuality.

"Are these marks tribal symbols?" she asked, continually

caressing the same section of black swirls and scrolls.

"I told a buddy of mine who's an artist I wanted markings with a tribal feel, but more artistic. So they don't mean anything specific."

"So it's wearable art that's unique to you." Her thumb swept across the stylized barbed wire motif on his bicep. "Even if the design was used on another person it wouldn't look the same. Your skin coloring gives it a different dimension. As does your musculature." She ran a fingernail on the underside of his arm. "Your biceps and triceps are amazing."

"I can't take credit for that."

"I'm pretty sure you weren't born with all these muscles." Maggie looked at him, as if startled by what she'd said.

When she attempted to remove her hand, Jon placed his palm over hers. "Thank you. Most of the time I get grief for the tats. I'm happy to hear a beautiful woman appreciates them."

"I do." She wet her lips and her gaze dropped to his mouth.

Sweet Jesus. She was killing him. Everything about her embodied soft and sweet—her hands, her mouth, her eyes, her tender touch. Which ironically enough, made him hard as a fucking drumstick.

"Maggie?" Seth called out.

They both jerked back.

"Yes, Seth?" she said a little breathlessly.

"Can you show Raven a couple of steps?"

Maggie said, "Sure," and stood. She faced him. "Truly magnificent, Jon."

"Glad you like them."

"I wasn't talking about the tattoos." Then she spun, leaving him staring after her.

Whoa. That comment had dripped with sexual sizzle.

Hmm. Maybe Maggie Buchanan wasn't as soft and sweet as he first believed.

JON SUCKED AT dancing. Like epically sucked.

The third night of class Seth and Maggie taught a waltz. Part of him feared they'd switched to an easier dance because he'd mangled the jitterbug the first two nights. Not that he could ask either instructor to give it to him straight, since Raven had hot-footed it out of class as soon as it ended. Then in the car the surly teen refused to talk to him and bailed out as soon as he'd pulled up to the curb in front of her house.

The fourth night was devoted to the rhumba. Jon wasn't the only one having troubles. Two other guys in his class—the quiet cowboy and the newlywed—suffered from the same feet, eye and hand coordination issues.

During the break, Jon saw the cowboy leaning against the wall by the drinking fountain. He struck up a conversation.

"You look ready to bolt for the door, man."

He nodded his black-hatted head. "Takin' a class together was my wife's idea, not mine."

"I hear ya. My niece roped me into this."

"At least you ain't gonna end up in divorce court if *you* quit," he grumbled.

Jon thrust out his hand. "Jon White Feather."

"Quinn McKay."

"Is your wife having a good time?"

"I guess."

Jon waited for the cowboy to complain more, but he wasn't much of a talker. He gulped down another mouthful of water and started to walk back, but the guy's voice stopped him.

"Know what I hate the worst?" Quinn said out of the blue.

"What's that?"

"I think I'm embarrassin' her."

"Right there with you."

Quinn lifted one dark eyebrow. "You gonna quit?"

Jon shook his head. "My niece is a teenager. I'd never hear the end of it. Besides, I'm too stubborn."

"Me too. I figure I'll get better. I sure as hell can't get any worse."

Jon laughed.

"If I wasn't so busy on the ranch I'd find a way to take private lessons. Then maybe my wife wouldn't look at me like

I've got the grace of a damn bear."

Seth motioned everyone back to class.

Jon managed not to tromp all over Raven's feet for the rest of class. But on the ride back to her parents' house after his disastrous attempt at the rhumba, Raven mentioned she was considering dropping the class and Jon knew he had to swallow what little pride he had left and ask for help.

"MAGGIE?"

Startled, she whirled around so fast she almost dropped her car keys. "Jon. You scared me. I thought you left."

"Sorry. I did. But I came back."

"Did you forget something?

"No." He jammed his hands in his pockets. As if he was nervous.

Right. She should be nervous after she'd cyber-stalked him and discovered he wasn't just some hot guy in a local band, but an internationally known and respected musician in a critically acclaimed band that incorporated traditional Lakota music with hard rock. "What's up?"

"I need your help. I'm a hopeless dancer. And while I find the humor in that, Raven doesn't. She's ready to quit because of me and I don't want to embarrass the poor kid any more than I already have. So I thought I'd see if you have time to give me a few private lessons."

Maggie hadn't been expecting that. Jon White Feather didn't seem like the type of guy who'd ask for help. She found it incredibly…sweet that he was more worried about his niece's feelings than projecting a macho reputation to the class. The problem was, she didn't have much free time. She'd gone from worried about having no job to being too busy to take on any extra projects.

But look at that project—you'd get to put your hands all over every tall, dark and handsome inch of that ripped, sexy body.

Jon stepped back. "Since you haven't said anything, I guess that's no."

She put her hand on his arm to stay his retreat. "It's not that. I'm just mentally dissecting my schedule to find a place where I might be able to squeeze you in."

"Any time you can give me would be great. I'm flexible."

"Any time? Even five o'clock in the morning?"

He grimaced. "Yep. Although I'll need plenty of bathroom breaks since it'll take at least a pot of coffee to wake me up at that god-awful time of the day."

"I was kidding." Maggie realized she was still touching him and dropped her hand. "You don't want Raven to know?"

"That I need remedial dance instruction? No. Only because she'd feel guilty for asking me to take her to these classes in the first place." Those intense blue eyes studied her. "I definitely don't want to put you on the spot with Seth, either."

Maggie frowned. Why would what Seth thought matter…? Oh. Jon assumed—like many people did—that dance partners were together. "Jon. Seth and I aren't a couple anywhere besides on the dance floor."

Was that relief in his eyes? "That's good to know. So what do you say? Will you help me fix at least one of my two left feet?"

"When you put it that way…" She smiled. "Seth and I practice for two to three hours after we're done teaching class. It'd be best if we scheduled it for directly after that."

"Two to three more hours? Damn. You sure you won't be tired?"

Probably. "Nah. I'll be fine."

"Okay. That'll work great. Thanks, Maggie."

"Don't thank me until I tell you how much I charge an hour."

"Worth every penny, I'm sure."

"I know we don't have class tomorrow night, but be here after eight and we'll get started."

"So you're giving Johnny-hottie private lessons?" Seth asked.

"Yes. Why?"

He fussed with the beaded sleeves on her dress. "Because I think he's faking it."

"Faking what? Stop tugging so hard."

"Sorry." Seth studied her hair critically. "With this dress you'll need an elegant hairdo. Not something cutesy with curls, but sleek and sophisticated."

It drove Maggie bat-shit crazy, how Seth expected her to follow three or four different conversations with him simultaneously. She snatched his hand. "Seth. What is Jon faking?"

"That he's a bad dancer. 'Cause, honey, ain't no one that bad. Especially not a drummer. And the man is always eating you up with those magnificent eyes of his, which leads me to believe he's faking it so he can be alone with you. He set the scene the first night. Now he's begging you to teach him on the sly? It's a classic ploy."

"Why doesn't he just ask me out?" Maggie countered. "We're both adults. Jon doesn't seem the type to play games."

Seth shrugged. "Maybe he's worried his niece will accuse him only of taking classes with her so he could pick up chicks. Maybe he's afraid a smoking-hot white girl like you won't date an Indian guy like him. Maybe he's so used to groupies throwing themselves at him he doesn't have a clue how to ask a normal woman out on a date."

Her partner's comments made perfect sense and yet…her

logical brain hadn't considered any of those reasons. "I guess we'll see, won't we?"

"No matter what his motives, I approve."

"You do?"

"Yes. Because if you happen to get naked with that man? Girlfriend, I expect explicit details." Seth reached into his magic bag of accessories and pulled out a hair clip. "Use this for now. I want to see how it looks with the costume."

Maggie bit back a groan as Seth cued up the music.

Taskmaster Seth didn't relent on rehearsal until Maggie literally cried "uncle" and broke away to get a drink.

Her lungs burned. Her feet hurt. She was sweating like crazy. Luckily she'd changed out of the costumes after the first full run-through. She glanced at the clock. Seth had been cracking the whip for two and a half hours.

"Are you throwing in the towel tonight, Maggie?" Seth asked.

"The towel that is soaked in sweat? Why, yes I am."

Footsteps echoed across the gym floor and they both turned.

Her heart, already beating madly, sped up at the sight of Jon, looking every inch the bad boy rocker, with his tousled dark hair, skintight black T-shirt, and faded, ripped jeans. And that smile. Good lord that fabulous smile was beyond sexy.

She drained half the bottle of water before she spoke. "You

made it."

"I've been here for a half hour watching you guys."

Seth bowed. "So what did you think?"

Jon's focus was entirely on Maggie. "Beautiful. Amazing. Graceful. Sexy." Then Jon looked at Seth. "And you weren't too bad either."

Maggie got the *I told you so* look from Seth.

"As much as I'd love to stay and chat, I still have to drive back to Rapid City tonight." Seth scooped up the costumes. "You'll deal with the audio stuff before you leave, Maggie?"

"Of course."

Seth bussed her cheek and whispered, "I slipped condoms in your dance bag." Then he faced Jon. "Ta, Johnny Feather. Get the moves right tonight for a change, okay?"

Her face flamed, but Jon just laughed. "Will do."

After the door slammed behind Seth, they looked at each other. She fought the urge to run. But she wasn't sure if it would be toward him, or away from him.

Jon invaded her space. "You look ready to bolt, Maggie. Have you changed your mind?"

"No."

He handed her a check. "For two lessons. I'll let you decide if I need more. Truthfully, I'm glad to hand you the reins and let you take the lead in this."

Her eyes searched his. "In this?"

"I'm used to being in charge of everything. Professionally and personally. Intimately." He flashed his teeth. "So take the lead while you can get it, teach. Because it ain't gonna last long."

There was a glimpse of his cocky side. "Prove it, little drummer boy."

Jon laughed—a sultry rumble that sent a delicious curl of heat through her. "How?"

"Rhumba. No music."

"So you *do* intend to torture me."

"Completely."

His first five moves were good enough that Maggie wondered if Jon had been exaggerating his bad dancing skills. But then everything fell apart. His body became board stiff. He high-stepped as if he was auditioning for a marching band. When he stomped on her foot for the third time, she retreated and bit back a wince. "Okay. We can't blame your rhythm issues on the music distracting you, since there is none."

"Well that's reassuring," he said tersely.

Maggie had an idea. "All right, let's see how you do dancing with a wall." She towed him to the back of the gym.

"Whoa. Hang on, doll face. You're joking, right?"

"Nope. Palms on the wall, about where you'd be holding my hands. Stand straight. Keep your feet shoulder-width apart. Stay just like that."

"I'm damn glad no one can see me because I feel ridiculous," he grumbled.

She ducked under his arms, pressing her back into the concrete blocks. "Do you trust me?"

Indecision flickered in his eyes.

Maggie set her hands on shoulders. "Jon. Do you think I'm purposely trying to make you feel ridiculous?"

He bit off, "No."

"Good. I *am* trying to help you."

"I know."

"Do you?" She set her hands on his chest. His rock-hard chest. His body was so warm. And ripped. She wondered if she could feel the cut of his abs through his thin T-shirt. Her fingers inched down…

"Maggie?"

What was wrong with her? She'd practically been feeling him up. "I can't help you if you won't let me."

Jon glanced down at her fingers digging into his pectorals. When his gaze met hers, his eyes held sexual heat. "I like this hands-on approach."

Lord, he could stoke the embers inside her to a five-alarm fire in three seconds flat. "Is this helping you?"

He offered her that slow, sexy smile. "It sure as hell ain't hurting me."

"Don't move. I'll start the music." She slipped away and

inhaled several deep breaths, trying to get ahold of her raging libido.

Jon hadn't budged an inch.

She couldn't help but sneak a look at Jon White Feather's backside. Yowza. Every bit as good as his front side. Damn, the man was fine. With a capital F. *Ogling his ass is not helping you control these urges, Maggie.* She stood behind him. "Now, I want to see those feet moving. Just like we've been working on. Ah ah ah, but I don't want you looking at your feet. Look straight ahead. As if you were gazing into your partner's eyes."

He nodded and shuffled his feet.

"That's awesome. Don't change anything."

But he did falter after another minute.

When Maggie curled her hands around his hips, tucking her body close behind his, he jumped forward. "Jesus, Maggie. What are you doing?"

"Teaching you. You said you liked the hands-on approach. I was trying to get you to use your hips."

Jon shot her a smug look over his shoulder. "Trust me, dancing queen, I *know* how to use my hips."

She imagined her hands gripping his biceps as he was propped above her naked, giving her firsthand knowledge of just how well he could move that pelvis.

"What's put that look on your face?" he asked softly.

Fighting a blush, she said, "Exhaustion," and stepped in

front of him. "Now count out the beat with me."

Strong fingers dug into her hips and he snugged his torso against hers—way too close. But she couldn't seem to tell him to back off.

"Feel how I move." Palms flat against the wall, she danced forward and back. "One, two. Three, four. One, two. Three, four. I don't hear you counting."

When his deep voice rumbled in her ear, she almost lost track of which damn number she was on.

"I'll face you and we'll do this for real. Don't change anything. Just keep counting." Maggie turned and his fingers drifted across her lower belly, sending her whole body on high alert.

Jon's eyes remained on hers as he slipped her hands into his. His husky voice repeated the numbers in a melodic cadence and the music faded into the background.

Forward. Back. His steps weren't perfect but his gait was much smoother.

She wondered how long they'd danced after the music ended. Something had shifted between them tonight. She attempted to pull away but Jon was having none of that.

"Thank you. I actually feel like I might not suck at this."

Maggie smiled. "You just need to be patient with yourself."

During the next half of the lesson, Jon even learned how to spin his partner and reverse steps. She was pleased with his progress and told him so.

Time passed quickly. But she had to get off her feet.

It took her longer than usual to pack up her stuff, but Jon wasn't inclined to leave. As much as she liked just talking to him, she suspected he'd stuck around out of obligation. "Jon. You don't have to stay. I don't want to keep you from your Friday night plans."

"I don't have any plans."

Tell him you don't either. Ask him to come over.

As good as that sounded…this week had drained her. Physically. Mentally. She wouldn't be good company. Heck, she'd probably fall asleep.

Jon asked, "What about your plans?"

"I plan on crawling into bed and not getting out until morning."

"What a coincidence. That's my favorite way to spend a Friday night too."

His meaning sent a dangerous shiver of longing through her. "You looking for an invite for a sleepover?"

He shrugged. "Never hurts to ask."

She stared at him, expecting he'd back off. Or at least take off.

But he didn't. He kept that penetrating gaze locked to hers. "I'll stick around until you're done. It's too late to be wandering around in a dark parking lot by yourself."

Jon did stick close as she checked both exits and entrances. Since the gym was a separate structure, the community center was already locked up.

He insisted on carrying her bag. He let his hand rest in the small of her back and she found her footsteps dragging on the jaunt to her car.

"I oughta pick you up and carry you," he grumbled. "You are dead on your feet."

What would it be like to have a big, strong guy whisk her into his arms?

Heavenly.

She sighed.

Then his warm mouth was on her ear. "You'd like that."

Yes. Yes she would. Too much. She stopped at her car and fiddled with her keys instead of meeting his gaze.

Thud. Her bag hit the ground. "Maggie." Jon inserted himself between her and the door, forcing her to look at him. "Come here."

"Jon. I'm okay."

"No you're not. Let me hold you up for a little while."

"But I shouldn't—"

"Just let go for a minute." He tugged her, gathering her in his arms. "I've got you."

Maggie melted into him, letting his warmth and strength flow through her. But her stomach made a loud gurgling noise and she reluctantly pulled away. "Obviously I skipped supper again."

"Then the least I can do is take you someplace to eat."

"That's sweet, but not necessary."

Then he was in her face. "You worked your ass off, you're hungry—so I *am* feeding you. Your choices are we go out, or I follow you home and cook for you there."

Maggie realized he wasn't taking no for an answer. She realized she really liked that about him. "All right. The Millstone is open. I'll meet you."

Four

JON CHOSE THE booth at the back of the restaurant and ordered coffee. After ten full minutes passed and Maggie hadn't shown, he wondered if he'd been stood up.

But that didn't seem like Maggie's style. Then again, what did he really know about her?

He knew she'd felt the same zing between them whenever their eyes met and whenever their bodies touched.

Then she swept into the restaurant. Her reddish-blond hair was still contained in a hair clip that showed off her elegant neck and stunning profile. She had the haughty look of classic ballerina in her angular facial features, and she exuded the grace of a dancer in the way she carried herself.

Jon was completely taken with her.

She slid opposite him. "Sorry. My car was on fumes so I had to fill up with gas." She picked up the menu and flipped through it. "What are you having?"

"All-day breakfast special number three."

"That sounds good."

The waitress took their order and Maggie looked at him expectantly. "Tell me about yourself, Jon White Feather."

"What do you want to know?" He braced himself for the intrusive personal questions people felt entitled to ask because he had a public persona as a musician.

"Your family. Where you got those stunning blue eyes."

Not what he'd expected, which was a good thing. And was she flirting with him? "Threw you, didn't they? Most folks assume I wear contacts. I don't. This eye color is courtesy of my mother."

"Don't take this the wrong way, but I suspected you weren't full-blooded Lakota. Your genetic makeup resembles Eden's more than your brother's."

"True. That's why Eden and I got along so well—we're both half-breeds. Jim's my half-brother. His mother died when he was young. My mother came to the Eagle Butte Reservation right after she graduated from college in Minnesota. She met my dad…"

"And your mom helped heal a widower's heart?"

"Ain't quite that romantic. Living on the rez wasn't as noble as it'd sounded in her sociology classes. Anyway, Jim is twelve years older than me. My brother Jared is four years younger than me. He's still giving our parents fits over his daredevil acts as a smoke jumper."

Maggie's brow furrowed. "Smoke jumper?"

"He travels all over the U.S. fighting wild fires with an elite group of all-Indian firefighters based out of Eagle Butte." He smirked. "Jared is hard to contain."

"Ha-ha."

"What about your family?" he asked.

"You know my brother Billy. I have an older sister Lacy who lives in New York with her husband and three kids. My dad died when I was in high school and my mom passed on a few years after I graduated from college. That's about it." She sipped her coffee. "How old are you?"

"Thirty-six. How old are you?"

"Thirty-two."

Jon knew he looked shocked. "Really?"

She bristled. "Yes. Why?"

"I thought you were like…twenty-six."

"Disappointed that I'm not a young, hot thing, rock star?"

He didn't bother to bank the heat in his eyes. "Not at all. Because *winyan*, you *are* a young, hot thing."

Maggie blushed. "What does *winyan* mean?"

"Woman. And you're all that."

"Flatterer. So tell me how you became Johnny Feather, international music star."

He snorted. "More like inter-*nation* music star. Entertaining American Indian tribes from the Arapahoe to the Zuni."

"But your band has traveled abroad, right?"

"Several times. Sapa spent four long months overseas last year."

"Doesn't sound like you had a good time."

"The performances were great. But we were sick of each other halfway through the tour. At least when we're here, we can go home to get away from each other. We've been touring for months on end, year after year. Sapa isn't booked for any paying gigs for a while. We're taking a long break." Maybe a permanent break.

Maggie looked at him curiously. "Is Sapa breaking up?"

Was she really that intuitive? Or was he just that transparent? He hedged. "Technically Sapa could go on even if half of us quit. The band has ten members. We rotate gigs for the lead guitarists and the bass guitarists because they have families. It's always worked. But the married members of the band, who aren't interchangeable, are expecting their first baby and wanted to be home for the summer and fall. Another member lost his father this spring and he quit because he has to take care of his mom full-time. The other couple called it quits in their relationship, and they're not sure they can work together professionally anymore."

"And what about you?" she prompted. "Are you interchangeable?"

"No. I'm key. I write the majority of our music. I've always dealt with the business end. The booking agents, the account-ants, the company putting on the tours and most of the media. If the band didn't like the venue, they blamed me. If we had to cancel or postpone a show, the booking agent blamed me. If we ran out of money mid-tour, the accountant blamed me. All I wanted to do was make music. My creativity has been totally tapped out because the last three years have been so stressful." Jon gave Maggie props for steering the conversation, but enough yammering on about himself. "What about you? Have you been overseas?"

"No. I always thought it'd be fun to go to the international dance competition world finals in London." She smiled. "I guess the regionals in Gillette in a few weeks will have to do."

"So that's why you're practicing all the time?"

"All the time is right. Evenings. Weekends. Hours of danc-ing. And that's after Seth has taught a full schedule at his dance studio and I've worked eight hours."

"Why do it?"

"Because I'm a sucker?"

Jon laughed softly. "No. Seriously. Do you love it that much?"

"Yes. I'd forgotten how much." She glanced out the win-dow. "After I graduated from college I was lucky enough to land a job in my field. I took a break from dancing, which turned into a few years' break."

"What is your day job?"

"Computer technology."

"So you're smart, beautiful and graceful? Now I'm really feelin' inadequate."

"At least you're not unemployed in your field," she grumbled. "Up until six months ago I worked for a computer security company that contracted civilian jobs on various military bases. Then budget cuts and corporate downsizing happened. I've been scrambling to stay financially afloat."

"I've definitely been there, done that."

"Struggling with finances? Or your career?"

"Both." Jon drummed his fingers on the table. "Starving artist is a reality in all the arts. I lived that hand-to-mouth lifestyle for many years. I'm happy to be past it. But now I'm struggling with fulfilling the creative side."

"Do you do that a lot?"

"Do what?"

Maggie dropped her hand over his fingers, still tapping out a beat on the table. "Use everything within reach as a drum?"

"Yeah. I guess I don't notice it." Then he had a flash of embarrassment. "Why? Is it annoying?"

"No. It's cute."

Cute. Awesome. He hadn't ever remembered being called cute.

"Have   you   done   anything   fun   since   the

band…disbanded?"

"Ha-ha, funny girl." Jon twisted his hand and threaded his fingers through hers. "I'm learning new moves from this sexy dance instructor I just met."

She blushed. But she didn't jerk her hand back.

Emboldened, he leaned forward. "Would you go out with me?"

Her pretty blue eyes searched his. "You'd want to go out with me? Seriously?"

"Yeah. Why not?"

"Because you're famous. You have gorgeous women all over the world falling at your feet. I did a little online stalking and I saw that picture of you and Desiree at some big music producer's house before your breakup."

Desiree—one name—was the up and coming darling of the indie rock world with ambition on becoming the "Indian Beyoncé". No doubt Desiree had talent; her voice was suited to a smoky blues style, pop or hard rock. She was a beautiful woman who proudly wore her Choctaw heritage. But Desiree had no intention of living her life out of the spotlight. She'd never settle down in South Dakota and he couldn't imagine settling anywhere else.

"The tabloids get a lot of shit wrong. I'm not nursing a broken heart over her. And here's where I point out that you're a gorgeous woman and I've fallen at your feet, more than once, in public, if I recall correctly."

She laughed. "My God. You are so smooth."

Jon brought her hand to his mouth and kissed her knuckles. "And sincere. And really happy you're here with me."

Their food arrived.

After Maggie devoured every morsel, she shoved her plate aside. "So about this date. When are you thinking?"

"You busy tomorrow night?"

"I'm free after rehearsal."

"Good. I'll pick you up…" Wait a second. He wasn't free. "I just remembered Saturday night won't work for me. Here I'm telling you Sapa is on break, but we're doing one set at the Heritage Bar. It's a benefit we agreed to months ago. But if you don't mind a late date, we can go out after I'm done." It'd be good for her to see him in action. Doing what he did best. Which wasn't dancing.

When Maggie hesitated, he cranked up the charm. "Come on. I deserve a chance to show you that I can keep a steady beat in some capacity."

"All right. It's a date."

"Excellent." Jon caught her trying to mask a yawn and he dropped cash on the table to cover the check. "Now that your belly is full, I don't feel guilty sending you home."

"I am fading fast."

Jon offered his hand to help her from the booth. He didn't

release his hold on her until they reached her car. "Thanks for the lesson tonight, dancing queen."

"My pleasure. What time should I be at your show?"

"We go on at eight. There might be a crowd—" an understatement, "—so maybe get there a little early."

"Where will I find you once you're done playing?"

Security would be tight around the stage, by the back door and the tour bus. "I'll meet you by the east side door. It might be as long as thirty minutes after the encore before you see me, so don't think I'm not coming. I will be there."

As much as Jon wanted to curl his hands around her face and take the kiss he craved, he settled for brushing his lips on her cheek. "Drive safe."

Five

MAGGIE'S FEET WERE killing her. Her body ached from holding dance pose after dance pose. Seth had run rehearsal today as a sadistic drill sergeant. Six hours with one fifteen-minute break.

She'd been so tempted to hobble home, soak her feet in Epsom salt and crawl in bed.

But when she'd turned on the radio in her car, the station was promoting the benefit concert. Then they played a couple of Sapa songs. And holy shit, it wasn't at all what she'd expected. She figured Sapa's musical style would be a cross between folk and instrumental, like those pan-flute playing South American Indians who annoyed the piss out of everyone at local fairs and festivals, with a few drums thrown in to call it hard rock.

Not so. Sapa rocked it hard, musically a mix of Godsmack, Evanescence and Alice in Chains. A primal tribal drum line alongside a chunky bass, and screaming electric guitars. The vocals alternated between male and female leads. Melodic one song, discordant the next, and punctuated with screamo sections any heavy metal fan could dig.

So there was no way she was missing it.

At her small cabin, she let the hot water soothe her sore muscles. After eating, she downed four aspirin and searched her closet for something edgy to wear.

Her job working for a civilian contractor on a rural Air Force base, sitting in front of a computer in a roomful of men, hadn't unleashed her inner fashionista. Pathetic to realize she didn't own anything funky or hip. Which made her feel…decidedly uncool.

At least the years dealing with hair and makeup in dance competitions allowed her to add a more dramatic look to her face. She shimmied on her favorite pair of jeans and a red camisole that'd shrunk in the washer; the shorter length did show some skin and her belly ring. After slipping on her red cowgirl boots, Maggie headed to the Heritage.

She'd given herself enough time, planning to arrive an hour early. The line to get in was unbelievably long. By the time she was inside, the place was wall-to-wall people and she couldn't get near the stage. But from what she could see, it'd be impossible to get past the multitude of security guards anyway.

It took fifteen minutes to flag down a cocktail waitress. Maggie checked her phone and saw she'd missed a call from Billy. Strange that he was calling her on a Friday night—

hopefully everything was all right. But it was too loud to hear his voice message now. She'd call him in the morning.

Finally the lights flickered off and on. The crowd's anticipation electrified the whole place. She found a spot against the far back wall where she had a view of the entire stage.

Chants of, "Sapa, Sapa," ended abruptly when the area in front of the stage went dark.

A man's high-pitched voice sliced through the air in traditional Native American chanting, singing without recognizable words. Another male voice joined in. And another. Then the steady *thump thump thump* of a drum. Deep tones that blended perfectly with the high notes. The sounds built and built…and then everything stopped.

The crowd collectively held its breath.

Then guitars and drums blasted from the stage, along with an explosion of light.

Maggie was absolutely blown away. One song segued into the next. A different style that showcased each musician's strength. She was a little shocked to see the person shredding guitar was a woman. When it came time to showcase the drummer, she was surprised when the stage hands rolled out another, completely different set of drums than the ones Jon had been using for the previous songs.

Jon jumped behind the new drum set and twirled his drumsticks above his head. The crowd roared when he began to play. The main beat was slow and steady. Very primal. The kind of deep thud that passed through her muscles and tissues and settled in to vibrate her bones. Her body tensed in anticipation for the next pulse. Then the next. And the next.

He layered a variety of drum jams—fast, syncopated, off-tempo, but no matter how quickly his drumsticks moved between drums, that first low, seductive beat never faltered.

No rhythm my ass.

Even when the guitars and voices joined in, turning the primitive beat into a song, Maggie felt the reverberation of the drum inside her body. Her pulse mimicked it. Her blood throbbed with it. She'd never had music affect her on such a visceral level.

She closed her eyes and imagined touching Jon, this primal rhythm in the background. Stroking him with her hands. With her mouth. Feeling the heat of his body as he rose above her. Feeling that hot, sweet throb of need as his flesh teased hers. Over and over. Until she was begging. Until they were joined and moving as one to the same rhythm.

That's when she realized her panties were slick. Lust burned through her so thoroughly that when she opened her eyes, she saw couples sating that same overpowering sexual need. Locked in a passionate kiss. Grinding and rubbing their bodies in sensual motion.

That jungle beat, hypnotic and strangely melodic, called to

her. She couldn't see Jon behind the wall of drums, but she felt his presence every time his drumstick connected with the drum skin.

The song ended and the band exited the stage. But the crowd wasn't ready to let them go. Maggie stomped her feet, ignoring the sting of pain, clapped her hands and whistled right along with them.

Several minutes later Sapa returned to the kind of deafening applause she was used to hearing in a stadium. The first encore song was a hard rock cover tune and Sapa knocked it out of the park. The second song was a stripped-down bluesy number, which morphed into an oddly compelling dissonant lullaby. The lead singer introduced the band members, the lights went up and the show was over.

Maggie wandered up to the bar, ordering a Coke and letting the crowd thin before she ventured outside. Security was still tight by the stage. As they moved the drum sets, Maggie wondered if Jon stayed backstage to supervise, or if his crew had done it so many times he didn't have to worry, and he was basking in fan adoration.

After finishing her drink, she wended her way through the people gathering for the next act, exiting out the side door. The night air cooled her cheeks, but did nothing to quell the heat burning inside her. Unused to the edginess, she paced. She spun and ran into a brick wall. A warm, flesh-and-blood brick wall.

She stepped back to apologize, but he spoke first.

"Maggie? Hey. I thought that was you. Sorry to keep you waiting."

She had to look away from his potent blue eyes. "You didn't. I just got out here." But her gaze dropped to his corded neck.

Do not imagine pressing your lips to the spot where his pulse is pounding as erratically as yours.

Jon didn't immediately speak. He didn't move either. Finally he asked, "Is everything all right?"

No. You practically gave me an orgasm just from hearing you play the drums.

"Maggie?"

Her hands had somehow landed on his chest and she squeezed his pecs.

"Why won't you look at me?"

"Because then you'll see," she said softly.

"See what?" His fingers were under her chin forcing her gaze to his. His focus moved from her eyes to her mouth, then back to her eyes.

"See that." She didn't have to put a name to it; the man recognized lust.

Curling his hand around the back of her neck, he brought their mouths together, only allowing a whisper-soft brush of his lips across hers. But each successive near-kiss silently urged her to part her lips. Then she could feel his breath in her mouth. A tease. A taste. She wanted more. Now.

When Maggie made a distressed sound, Jon consumed her mouth in a kiss that robbed her of reason. A kiss packed with passion as his tongue invaded her lips, licking into her mouth. Cranking her desire to fever pitch as he proved he was a man in complete command. He situated her head to deepen the kiss to his liking. The tips of his fingers—so adept at creating hard driving music—stroked her jawline in the perfect mix of rough and tender.

She pressed her body to his, wishing for a solid surface behind her so she could twine her arms and legs around him.

Almost as if he'd read her thoughts, he propelled her backward until her spine connected with the building. He gripped her ass and lifted her, his pelvis held her in place as his hands roamed. Every spot he touched made her purr. Made her arch. Made her dizzy and greedy. Her hands dove into his hair, twining the silky damp strands around her fingers.

If a kiss was this mind-blowingly explosive, sex with this man would be off the charts.

Jon slowed the pace from frantic to flirty. Interspersing long, hot kisses with sweet, affectionate pecks. A tug of his teeth on her lower lip. Or her earlobe. A fleeting flick of his tongue on those same spots. Then that wicked mouth skated over her neck. Sucking. Licking. Biting.

She moaned when he placed his open mouth on the swell of her breast. "Don't stop."

He rested his forehead in the curve of her shoulder, his breathing ragged. "We have to stop. I'm not gonna maul you out here where anyone can see us."

Maggie dug her fingers into his scalp until he lifted his head and looked at her. "Then take me someplace private and I'll let you maul me all you want."

He released her. Once her feet were on the ground, he clasped her hand and led her by the tour buses.

At seeing the crowd, she panicked for a moment and hung back.

Jon spun around to face her. "Are you changing your mind?"

"No. But there are so many people. And I don't…" Want to be just another groupie you bang after a show on your tour bus.

He correctly read her anxious expression. "I'm not taking you to my bus. I'm taking the shortcut to my car."

"Oh."

When he kissed her again with a mix of authority and seduction she was lost to everything but how right his arms felt around her. How perfect his mouth fit against hers.

"Jon?"

The surprising sound of her sister-in-law's voice had her ripping her mouth from Jon's and turning around.

Eden and Billy stared at them in complete shock.

Then her hotheaded brother grabbed Jon's arm. "Jesus, Maggie. *You're* out here sucking face with White Feather?"

Jon didn't acknowledge Billy at all. Keeping his gaze locked to Maggie's, he said to Billy, "Get. Your. Hand. Off. Me."

"Billy," Eden said, "you're causing a scene. Let him go."

He listened to his wife, but kept his focus on Maggie. "I want to know what the hell you're doing with him."

Maggie raised her chin. "Hi, Billy. Nice to see you too. I see you know Jon."

"Yeah, I know Jon. But my question is do *you* know him?"

"What is your problem?"

"That." Billy gestured to the women gathered around the tour buses. "Because that's who he is. Johnny Feather. His fuck 'em and leave 'em reputation doesn't bother you?"

Jon swore and lunged at Billy, but Eden inserted herself between the men.

"Jon. Back off. And you—" Eden poked Billy in the chest, "—leave it alone. This is not our concern."

Maggie wondered why Billy had overreacted. He never pulled the *I'm your big brother* bullshit when it came to her relationships. There had to be more going on here, but this wasn't the time or place to find out.

Eden faced Jon. "So, the reason we tracked you down, Jon, was to tell you awesome show tonight." She stroked her hand over her rounded belly. "Even the papoose was rockin' out in here."

"How are you feelin'?" Jon asked, giving Eden a soft smile.

"Fat. Happy." She shot her husband a sideways glance. "Most of the time. But it is past our bedtime and we'll be goin' home."

A fuming Billy looked at Maggie. "Need a ride?"

"I'm good. But thanks."

The other band members exited the back door. A group of fans broke free from security on the opposite side and they were surrounded.

Jon let go of Maggie's hand, stepping in front of her, but people moved between them—and Maggie got pushed back by the doors.

It was total chaos. She jumped up and down, waving to try and get Jon's attention, but he had his back to her. When she finally caught a glimpse of his face, he was deep in conversation with someone.

He hadn't been looking for her at all.

Disappointment dogged her. She scoured the crowd to see if Billy and Eden had escaped, but mostly to make sure they hadn't seen that Jon had forgotten about her. She also didn't want her pain-in-the-ass brother to think he'd been right.

On the long walk back to her car, Maggie realized she hadn't given Jon her phone number. The fact he couldn't call her didn't bother her as much as the thought she would've slept with him without them exchanging basic information. That was so unlike her. She'd practically done a full background check on other guys she'd just considered dating.

By the time she'd reached her cabin, she'd almost convinced herself the interruption from her brother and the crowd had been for the best.

Almost.

Six

JON WOULDN'T SAY he stormed into Billy Buchanan's office on Monday morning, but the new secretary working at Feather Light might argue that point. And she did.

"I tried to stop him, but he wouldn't listen," she huffed, following Jon into the room.

Billy looked up from the drafting table, his eyes decidedly frosty. "It's okay, Dani. This is Jim's brother. Evidently that entitles him to walk into whatever office he wants, whenever the hell he feels like it."

"Would you like me to tell Jim his brother is here?" she asked.

Jon and Billy said "no" simultaneously.

Dani slunk out and shut the door behind her.

Billy moved from behind the drafting table and pointed to the chairs in front of his desk. "Sit."

Jon preferred to stand. And pace. So he could take a swing at Billy if he got the chance.

Tough talk. He wouldn't do it. Not because this was his brother's partner, but he'd left his fighting days behind him.

He watched Billy, trying to find a family resemblance between him and Maggie. Same blue eyes. Same blond tones in their hair, although Maggie had more red in hers. Besides that, they looked nothing alike. Acted nothing alike either.

Billy seemed to be scrutinizing him too. "So, you're here because you're pissed off about what I said Saturday night?"

"Do ya think? Where do you get off—"

"She's my fucking sister! She deserves better than you."

"Because I'm Indian?" Jon had clenched his jaw so tightly he wasn't sure how the words had forced themselves out.

Billy shook his head. "Race has nothing to do with this. And fuck you for even bringing that up. I'm married to an Indian woman and our child will be mixed race. My partner is Indian. My sister Lacy's husband is part Indian. The goddamn color of your skin plays no part in it."

"Then what?"

"You really need me to spell it out for you? You use and discard women. A different city, a different girl every night. That's not hearsay, Jon. You yourself told me that. So I'm just supposed to smile and say nothing when I see you practically fucking my sister in public?"

Jon tapped his fingers on the armrest. "Number one, I wasn't 'practically fucking' Maggie; I was kissing her. Number two, you sure your feelings aren't misplaced out of guilt? You don't want me around your sister because you're afraid I'll tell her that we had a threesome…with your wife?"

Billy glared at him.

"I'm not off base, am I?" Jon prompted.

"Fuck. Maybe that is part of it." Billy ran his hand through his hair and muttered, "We can't change the past."

"But we sure as hell can hide it, right?"

"I'd hoped that would be a given."

Jon shrugged. "I haven't told anyone, because contrary to what you believe, I don't blab about my sex life." When Billy started to contradict him, Jon held up his hand. "And please don't pretend you think you know me, based on that one time we stayed together in the condo, for two days, over four years ago."

Billy snorted. "You saying you've changed?"

"I'm saying what we talked about, how much pussy I was getting back then was brought up by you—not me. I won't deny I've taken what was freely offered to me. Does that make me a man whore? No doubt. But I take offense to your statement that I use and discard women. I don't."

"Maybe that's the way you see it, or how you justify it. But I watched you Saturday night. Within minutes of being surrounded by adoring fans, Johnny Feather forgot about Maggie Buchanan entirely. She tried to get your attention but you didn't see her. Know what sucked about that? I had to witness the disappointment on her face. I tried to prevent my sister from getting hurt and it happened anyway."

Jon hated that Billy was right on that point. He hadn't realized Maggie hadn't hung around until the crowd had thinned and everyone had gotten a piece of him.

"Go ahead and call me a dick for saying this, but I'm glad Maggie saw that side of your life—of you—before you two get more involved."

And what really stung? Jon wished Billy was wrong, but he wasn't sure he was.

"Did you call her and apologize?" Billy asked.

"I don't have her phone number." He scowled. "And I wasn't about to call you or Eden to get it."

"Smart choice." Billy leaned back in his chair. "Make another smart choice, Jon. Walk away from her."

I don't know if I can. "I'll remind you that Raven and I are taking dance lessons from Maggie and Seth."

"I wish Eden wouldn't have suggested Maggie teach that dance class. It's just giving her false hope about returning to dancing when she needs to look for a real full-time job."

"Jesus, Billy. Have you actually said that bullshit to Maggie?"

"What's wrong with telling her the truth?"

"That's not the truth. That's crushing her dream and her

spirit. Maggie loves dancing and she's damn good at it. Why shouldn't she have a chance to do something that she loves?"

Billy leaned forward. "Because it is a dream. Dreams don't pay the bills and provide for the future. I'm sure you're telling her something completely different, you creative types don't tend to be grounded in reality. But Maggie is. She had a great job and a great career. That dance partner has filled her head with pipe dreams. She'll just end up disappointed again."

"Again?"

"Like in college. She got to the point her dance schedule affected her academics. I sat her down and talked to her about her future, telling her the best she could've hoped for with a performance degree was to end up teaching. She buckled down in a field of study that would be financially rewarding and stabilizing, made decent grades and ended up with a better-than-average job right after graduation."

Jon kept his mouth shut. But his gut clenched, thinking of the joy on Maggie's face when she danced. And the wistful look when she'd told him how much she'd missed that part of herself. What would Jon have done if his brother had sat him down and told him not to pursue a music career? Because Jon respected Jim so much, he would've listened.

Luckily Jim had backed Jon one hundred percent. Neither his siblings nor his parents had projected their life goals and expectations on him and he was grateful for that. More grateful than ever, now that he understood how rare that was. Jon didn't doubt Billy had done it out of love and concern for Maggie. But it broke his heart a little that she'd just given up.

The intercom on Billy's phone buzzed. "Yes?"

"Jim said to tell his brother he wants to see him in his office when you're done with him."

"Will do, Dani. Thanks." Billy cocked his head. "So we done?"

"Yep." Jon got up and walked out. Straight to his car. Jim would be pissed he'd ignored him, but he'd deal with it later.

Right now he just needed to think.

Mid-afternoon, Jon's cell rang. The call wasn't from his brother, as he'd expected, but his agent. "Johnny-boy! How are ya, kid?"

Kid. Anyone under forty qualified as a kid in Marty Goldman's world. "I'm all right. What's up?"

"I'll cut right to the chase. Someone from *Indie Rock* magazine was at Sapa's show in Spearfish Saturday night."

"Yeah? Why's that matter?"

"Because she heard rumors that the band is going on hiatus indefinitely."

Jon paced to the big window in the living area. "Not a rumor, Goldman, as you know."

"That's what I told her yesterday. So is it a coincidence that today I get a call from Darkly Dreaming's management company? They're auditioning drummers. They want to talk to you."

"Whoa. Wait a damn second. I'm on hiatus too. Remember our conversation about me being tired of touring and having no life? That hasn't changed."

"Which I understand. But damn, kid, Darkly Dreaming is big time."

"I don't care. I'm burned out. I need this time off."

An exasperated sigh echoed in his ear. "It's almost been a month."

"That's the longest break I've had in years and it hasn't been near long enough." Jon rubbed his forehead against the impending headache. Did his agent understand him at all? Or did he just see dollar signs? "Tell them I appreciate their interest but no thanks."

"That mean you don't want to know who else is expressing interest in you?"

Fuck. Marty just had to dangle another carrot, didn't he? "Who?"

"Push and Radioactive Tar are also auditioning drummers."

Holy shit. He'd kill to work with Van Conner, who produced Push and had scored a Grammy on their last CD.

Radioactive Tar was a group of studio musicians in Nashville that had a rotating roster of who's who in music. Just making contact with any one of those bands could give a big boost to his music career.

But you're taking a break, right?

"Kid? You still there?"

"Yeah. Just picking my jaw up off the floor."

"I thought you might say that," he said smugly. "But here's the catch. All of them want to set it up for this week."

Dammit. He had dance class with Raven in four hours. "Is there any way we can get it postponed for another week?"

"Nope. In fact, Push wants the meeting in Seattle tomorrow night."

As much as he still needed a break from his hectic lifestyle, meeting with these bands wouldn't be like touring and promoting. It would be about music. His music. No harm in hearing what they had to say, was there?

His artistic subconscious sneered at him for being fickle, accusing him of missing the rock-star life of fawning fans and fame. Throwing in a final jab about lying to himself and everyone else about settling down.

But his practical side warned him opportunities like this didn't come along every day and he'd be a fool to let it slip away.

The phone clunked. Paper rattled. Marty sighed. "I hate to

pressure you, but my secretary says there's one seat left on the nine o'clock flight to Denver tonight leaving out of Rapid. And the flight from Denver to Seattle puts you in Seattle around midnight."

He'd figure out something to tell Raven—just as soon as he made sense of his decision himself. "That'll work. Have your secretary book me at the Cooper Hotel in downtown Seattle."

"Done. I'll have her book your flights to L.A. and Nashville to meet with the other bands. Call me in the morning and I'll give you all the details. But remember; keep a lid on this, kid." Marty hung up.

Jon showered, packed and closed up his house, although he wouldn't be gone more than a week. While getting ready, he'd come up with a possible solution to his dance class dilemma. Or at least, he had an idea who could help him. He paced while he was waiting for her assistant to ring him through.

The line clicked. "This is Eden Buchanan."

"Knock, knock, knocking on Eden's door…"

"Jon, you magnificent bastard. I miss you serenading me."

"Doubtful, or you would've picked me over old what's-his-face. Still… How is it you look more beautiful now that you're knocked up? It pains me to admit you'll always be the woman I let slip through my fingers. The gold standard that I hold all other women to."

She laughed. "That sweet talking means one thing… What do you want?"

"A really big—and we're taking huge—favor…"

Seven

THE WEEK HAD started out on a bad note and had gone downhill from there.

Maggie had ended up working extra time at the doctor's office when they had a security breach with their server. She'd fixed it, but it was a pointed reminder that she missed the challenge of working in her field and not just killing time doing data entry.

Seth had been in a lousy mood all week, which hadn't made rehearsing fun. When she called her BFF Sara, who was also Seth's sister, to ask what was going on, Maggie ended up confessing her problems and the perplexing situation with Jon. She and Sara dissected it ten different ways and neither could come up with a plan besides to let it ride.

Maybe Maggie was a fool to think there was something there besides a few sexy looks, hot touches and stolen kisses, but that didn't stop her from hoping she'd see him again, either in class or outside of it.

Right now, she had a bigger problem. She turned the key in the ignition one more time and heard nothing but clicks.

"Piece of shit car." Maggie banged her fists on the steering wheel.

Of course it had to be pouring rain. Not the warm, summertime showers, which were a welcome relief after a scorching day. No, the wind blew so hard it shook her little car. The inside of the windows were so fogged up she could barely see her headlights.

That was a good sign, wasn't it? That the headlights were working even if they were dim? When she reached forward to wipe off the condensation, she accidentally laid on the horn and spooked herself good.

Get a grip, Maggie.

She unplugged her cell phone from the car charger and groaned. Even her cell was dead. Looked like she had no choice but to go back into the gym and call a cab.

Just as she turned to open her car door, she noticed a hooded figure peering in her window. She screamed and scrambled into the passenger's seat, thoughts of psychotic killers disabling cars in deserted parking lots running through her brain.

The door opened and the hooded figure's head was inside the car. "Maggie? It's me."

"Jon? What are you—"

"I was driving by and I saw your car was still here. Is everything okay?"

"No. My car won't start and I don't know what's wrong with it."

"It's pouring out here too damn hard for me to take a look." He held out his hand. "Come on. I'll get you home."

Touching him released a pulse pounding rush of sexual awareness, and she knew by the dark look in his eyes he felt it too.

Maggie grabbed her stuff and made a mad dash for Jon's vehicle, but she was still soaked to the skin when she climbed inside.

Jon shoved her bag in the backseat. "It's a frog strangler out there, eh?"

She shivered. "I won't complain because we need the rain, but doesn't it just figure I'd have car trouble tonight."

He reached over, letting his thumb sweep over her jawbone.

Maggie shivered harder, but she didn't jerk away. "What?"

"You splashed mud on your face."

"Thanks." She stared at him. "You missed class this week."

"I had to deal with band stuff."

That was evasive.

"Raven didn't tell you?"

"No, she was pretty enamored with her substitute partner."

Jon frowned. "I would've called you directly to let you know but I didn't have your number."

Or you were avoiding me after that steamy kiss Saturday night and the run-in with my brother.

She waved him off. "Doesn't matter."

"It does to me. Look, Maggie—"

"Forget it. I'm tired, wet and I just want to go home. I do appreciate you rescuing me tonight, so thanks."

"No problem." Jon started the vehicle and paused at the parking lot exit. "Which way?"

"Left. I live out on Burner Road."

Rain fell in sheets, so heavy at times Jon slowed to a crawl on the city streets. "I don't know that I've ever seen it rain this hard."

Maggie peered out the side window. Water was running over the gutters and at least six inches of water covered the city streets. "Me either."

"My brother would make a crack about the tribe's rain dances finally working. I'll bet the creek is running high."

Creek. She hadn't even thought about that. "Dammit."

He shot her a glance. "What?"

"The only way to get to my place is over Burner Bridge and it crosses the creek."

Jon pulled into a parking lot. "That's a problem. Too dangerous to try and cross it now, either on foot or by car."

She knew he was right, but that further limited her options. It'd be rude to show up and Billy and Eden's place this late, without calling. Chances were high all the hotels were full since they were in the height of tourist season. Her friends lived in Rapid City.

"I know this puts you in a bind. So if you want, you can stay with me. I have an empty guest bedroom. Tomorrow morning I'll bring you back and maybe I can figure out what's wrong with your car."

Alone. With Jon White Feather. All night. This would definitely be a test of willpower.

"If you're worried I'm gonna tie you up with duct tape, call Eden and Billy so they know where you are."

That conversation wouldn't go well since Billy had already warned her off Jon. Plus, Maggie would be mortified to make the call—she was a thirty-two-year-old woman, not a sixteen-year-old girl reporting in that she was breaking curfew. "The phone call isn't necessary. If you do decide to tie me up, I hope you use something besides duct tape. That gummy residue is a bitch to scrub off skin."

He was shocked for a millisecond before he granted her that sexy smile. "Good to know."

They didn't speak for the rest of the drive, unless she counted him muttering about the lousy visibility and horrible road conditions.

He veered off to the right onto a gravel road outside of Spearfish Canyon. The Black Hills spruce trees formed a canopy above them, softening the deluge. When they reached a big iron gate, he pointed a remote control device at the box on the fence post and the gate swung open.

"Wow. Fancy."

"It discourages pesky relatives, door-to-door salespeople and bible thumpers who want to save my eternal soul."

Maggie suspected it also kept out fans, or groupies, or whatever they were called.

Water had pooled in spots in the road, turning it into a mud bog.

Jon dropped it into four-wheel drive and said, "Hang on," before he gunned it.

They bumped up a hill and when it leveled out she caught her first glimpse of the place he called home. Security lights illuminated a ranch-style log house with a small deck on the front and a two-car garage on the far left side. "This place is so well lit."

"The security system attached to the gate alerts me if someone enters through it. The sensors tell me if someone tries to get around it on foot."

"Got a stockpile of valuables you're protecting?"

"Nope. Just my privacy." He poked the garage door opener clipped to the visor.

"You sure I won't be intruding?"

He stopped the vehicle halfway through the garage door and turned to look at her. "I wouldn't have asked you to stay with me tonight if I wasn't sure."

That could be taken a couple of different ways.

Maggie whistled after they'd parked. "This is the cleanest garage I've ever been in. How long have you lived here?"

Jon grabbed her bag from the backseat. "Three years. It's clean because I haven't been here that much."

He kept his hand on the small of her back as they exited the garage into a mud room. He set her bag on the washer, unzipped his hoodie and tossed it in a big sink.

Oh man. Her mouth dried seeing the wet T-shirt clinging to every muscle of his upper arms and chest. This man had such a beautiful body. Well-defined arms, contoured pecs, flat stomach. He unlaced his hikers and peeled off his socks, dropping them in the sink. He glanced up at her. "I freakin' hate wet socks."

Don't you hate wet shorts too? Maybe you oughta strip off those camo shorts so I know firsthand whether you're a boxers or briefs guy.

When her gaze met his, his startling blue eyes danced with amusement. "Do you have dry clothes in your bag?"

"Nothing besides dance clothes."

"I'll lend you something. I'll show you to your room."

Maggie had the impression of bright colors and Native American artwork as he led her down a long hallway. He opened the second door and flipped on the lights. "The bathroom is through that pocket door. Hang tight for a sec and I'll grab some clothes."

She had time to wander the cozy room, with its terra-cotta-colored walls and vibrant turquoise accents. The queen-size bed faced a window, although it was too stormy to see the view.

Jon was back before she ventured into the bathroom. "My former tour manager left these on the bus and somehow they ended up at my place." He passed her a pair of neon yellow Capri sweatpants and a gray tank top with Sapa emblazoned across the front.

"Thanks." Maggie's bra and underwear were fairly dry so she didn't have to go commando beneath the borrowed clothes. She tracked Jon to the kitchen. Not an ostentatious space, but homey. A cooktop was in the center island, which was surrounded by a horseshoe-shaped eat-in counter and six leather barstools. Lightning flashed above her head. She glanced up at the reflection in four enormous skylights. "Those are great."

"Jim knows I like to look at the stars, so he designed this house with that in mind." He took a sip of bottled water. "Would you like something to drink? Water, soda, iced tea.

I'm not much for alcoholic beverages, but there's probably a bottle of wine rolling around here someplace."

"Water is fine. Although it seems silly to be thirsty when I was just drenched to the skin." She was still shaking, but she was beginning to think it wasn't from the cold. The heated way Jon looked at her should be setting her blood on fire.

"I'll show you around the rest of the house while I still can. Electricity can be wonky out here during storms." He hit a switch, flooding the living area with light.

The furniture faced a brick fireplace that took up almost the entire back wall. A coffee table crafted from a gnarled tree root was centered on top of a vivid rug, patterned with Native American symbols. When Maggie ran her hand along the back of the couch, her fingers encountered baby soft leather. "I could just curl into this couch and doze off."

"Go ahead. I spend a good chunk of my time with my feet up, staring aimlessly upward."

After she'd stretched out, she noticed a glass ceiling that nearly spanned the length of the room. "Holy shit."

"That's what the insurance company said when I applied for a homeowner's policy," he said dryly. "I love it, but it does have drawbacks. Luckily there's a retractable metal covering, so if something happens while I'm out of town, my house wouldn't be open to the elements and the critters for months on end."

"I wish I could see the stars."

He moved behind her and dimmed the lights.

"Do you have a telescope?"

"Nope." He sat on the edge of the coffee table, his forearms resting on his thighs. "I prefer looking with the naked eye."

I'd prefer you looking at me naked with those sexy eyes of yours.

Another smirk curled the corners of his mouth, making her wonder if she'd said that last thought out loud. "So you're an amateur astronomer?"

"Not really. It's not even a hobby. Just something I do for relaxation and fun. What about you?"

"Meaning…do I have hobbies?"

"Meaning…what do you do for relaxation and fun?"

"I haven't indulged in my favorite way to relax for a long time."

Pause. Then, "Now you've aroused my interest."

When she realized how suggestive that sounded, she blushed to the roots of her hair. Wait. Had he said aroused?

He chuckled. "The fact you're blushing gives me all sorts of ideas on how you like to relax. And if I can help you out with that, just let me know."

Yes, please.

Rain pattering on the glass made a soothing sound. After a bit she said, "I'm surprised you don't have a TV in here."

"I'm not a fan of how media has overtaken every part of day-to-day life. It's like no one can stand silence."

"Before I lost my job I was always too busy to pay attention to a pretty sunset or a wren warbling in a tree. But now even if Seth keeps me dancing until ten o'clock at night, I make time to empty my head. Just me and nature."

Jon reached for her hand and kissed the tips of her fingers. "You're not at all like I imagined you'd be the first day I saw you teaching dance class."

"Really?"

"Really. And I meant that in a good way." He rubbed his thumb over her knuckles. "You looked every inch the prima ballerina. Beautiful, graceful. I expected temperamental, which I haven't seen. An uppity white girl, which I haven't seen either. Passionate, which I've had just a little taste of."

She held her breath, waiting for him to say he wanted to see more of that side of her.

But Jon just kept his compelling blue eyes on hers. "You want a tour of the house?"

"Ah, sure."

Keeping hold of her hand, Jon skirted a large sculpture of an eagle soaring into the sky with a fish clutched in its talons.

They walked past her guest bedroom and he showed her another empty room, which held two sets of bunk beds. "My nephews and nieces stay here a lot when I'm home."

How sweet that he was so involved in their lives. The next door was set back about ten feet from the hallway. "That's the den. There's where you'll find the flatscreen, DVD player, gaming consoles, foosball table, dart board. Typical single-guy stuff."

"Do you spend much time in there?"

"Depends on how long I've been on the road. But I usually only hang out in there when someone comes over."

Maggie poked her head inside. Everything looked brand new. He must not do much entertaining.

Jon dropped her hand and faced her at the last door. "This is my bedroom."

"Do I get to see it?"

"Depends on if it makes you uncomfortable when I admit I've imagined you in my bed since we first met. That said, I didn't offer you a place to stay so I could sweet talk you into a tumble between my sheets."

Outwardly she stilled, but inside her heart galloped and her stomach did pirouettes. When he stepped aside to allow her into his room, she murmured, "Well, that's a shame."

Maggie took in the king-size bed, the dressers, more big windows, covered with draperies. She peered into the adjoining bath, done in black and chrome. Then she wandered out and perched on the edge of the bed. "Bet you're happy to come home to this place after being on the road."

Jon still leaned in the doorway, arms crossed over his chest. "Yep. And today is one of the rare days I've made my bed."

"You sound proud of that."

"I am."

"Is this where I finally get a glimmer of rock-star behavior?"

He smiled. "Maybe. I stay in hotels and the maids clean up after me. I stay in the tour bus and we have a service that cleans it or I sleep on an unmade bunk. I tend to forget I'm responsible for those mundane things when I come home."

Her fingers pleated the plush comforter fabric as she tried to figure out how to phrase her next question. "Your house is great but I expected—"

"It to be bigger? More ostentatious?"

"No. I expected you to have a music room."

Jon's posture relaxed. "I have an entire studio behind the house. You didn't see it when we drove up?"

She shook her head.

"I wanted to keep the spaces separate. One where I could work on music and write. And a home where I could just be."

He sauntered forward with that sex-on-legs walk and she couldn't look away from him.

Then he gently pushed her shoulders and she rolled down onto the mattress. He loomed over her. "So we staying in here and messing up the sheets? Or returning to the living room for polite conversation?"

His pupils were so dark she couldn't see any blue in his eyes. He radiated enough body heat any chill on her skin evaporated. This potent, sexy man wanted her. *Her.*

Maggie wreathed her arms around his neck. "Fuck polite. Let's get wild."

Eight

JON LOST HIS focus for a moment as he kissed her, cranking the heat simmering between them into an inferno.

Maggie's body arched, one hand twisted in his hair, the other gripping his hip. Her soft lips clung to his as her tongue stroked and teased, her mouth urgent in expressing her need.

He pushed up and looked down at her.

Seeing the flush on her cheeks and the passion darkening her eyes almost had him throwing caution to the wind, giving into the hard, fast fuck they both wanted now and slowing it down for a second round.

But Maggie wasn't taking the lead in this dance.

"I like seeing you in my bed," Jon said silkily, pressing a kiss below her ear. Then he let his lips follow her jawline to the other ear. "But I'd like it even more if you were naked."

"Have I mentioned how fast I am at getting in and out of my clothes? I can show you if you want."

He smiled against her cheek. "Nope. Because we're doing

this my way."

"Meaning slow."

"Meaning…my way." Jon rubbed his mouth over hers, keeping their eyes locked, which increased the intimacy of the connection.

Maggie undulated beneath him, her impatience palpable.

"Got some place to be?" he asked.

"On top of you, riding you like a pony."

"That's something we'll have to try. Later." He captured her mouth with a kiss packed with such sexual greed, she whimpered when he broke free. Jon scooted forward on his knees, forcing her to straddle his legs. "Lift your arms."

She sat up and he removed the tank top.

Jon curled his hands over her shoulders, sweeping his thumbs across her clavicle. "So pretty."

"If I'd known I'd end up here tonight, I would've worn something sexier than my sports bra."

He tipped her chin up. "Ask me tomorrow what bra you wore and I won't remember. But I will remember the taste of your skin and how it felt when I touched you. Take it off."

Maggie pulled her bra off and flopped back on the bed. "Now it's easier for your hands to fulfill the promises that sweet-talkin' mouth of yours just made."

"And fulfill they will."

She gestured to his shirt. "You are lagging behind."

"Can't have that." Jon performed a slow striptease with his sleeveless T-shirt as he removed it.

Her eyes ate up his chest, arms and abdomen once he was completely bared to her. "God. I want to lick every one of your tattoos."

"In time." He hovered above her chest, his hot breath drifting over her damp skin. Then he dipped his head and his hair fell forward, brushing the upper swells of her breasts and the puckered tips of her nipples.

She hissed when his wet tongue lashed a tight point. "I'll give you about an hour to stop doing that."

Jon chuckled. "I'll promise I'll pay them the proper respect next time. I've got something else in mind for now."

His hair zigzagged across her belly as he scooted down her body. He teased and tormented her until she writhed. Finally he tapped her hip and when she lifted up, he peeled off her sweatpants.

She was gorgeous naked. Firm muscles beneath her ivory skin. A small strip of strawberry-blond curls striped her mound, leading to that sweet, pink pussy.

Jon reached for her hand. He nuzzled her wrist and his mouth moved upward, kissing the center of her palm before he sucked her middle finger completely into his mouth.

Maggie hissed. She'd propped herself up on both elbows and studied him from beneath lowered lashes, her body so restless he could feel sexual energy emanating from her.

He released her finger and placed the wet tip over her clit. "Show me how you touch yourself."

Her cheeks flushed with color. "Shouldn't you be doing that?"

"I'll do more than watch, trust me."

At first Maggie was self-conscious. But when Jon murmured encouragement and started trailing the backs of his fingers over her thighs, she gave herself over to self-pleasure. Swirling circles around that nub. Flicking it lightly. Watching his eyes, she slowly pushed her middle finger into her opening. She rocked her wrist back and forth, grinding the heel of her hand against her clit.

As soon as she removed her finger, Jon bent down and sucked it, releasing a tiny growl at his first taste of her. After he'd licked away all the sweet juice, he demanded, "Again."

Maggie glided her fingertip up and down her slit, adding more cream before vigorously rubbing her clit in a side-to-side motion. A moan escaped and she plunged her finger into her pussy, bumping her hips up to drive that digit in deeper.

Jon's erection dug into his stomach when he dropped to the mattress. But he ignored the pain and latched onto Maggie's butt cheeks, pulling her sex against his mouth. He thrust his tongue into her pussy alongside her finger.

"Oh God."

He scraped his teeth over her knuckle. "Move your hand." As soon as she complied, his thumbs spread open her swollen sex. He licked and sucked every inch of her intimate flesh, feasting on her.

Maggie had clamped her hands to his head as she thrashed beneath him. She jerked his scalp after he'd lightly grazed her clitoris with his teeth. "Sorry."

"Don't be," he growled. "It turns me on when you pull my hair." He used the very tip of his tongue to flick across that distended nub. She made sexy whimpering mewls and he fastened his lips to the pliant, throbbing skin and sucked.

"Keep doing—yes, just like that." Her body seized up and he felt the climactic pulses against his mouth.

After Maggie's legs quit twitching and the pressure on his scalp disappeared, he placed a soft kiss above her mound. He pushed off the mattress, ditched his shorts and rolled on a condom.

Their eyes met and then he was on her, in her. Thrusting into that tight, wet, hot cunt.

She locked her ankles on his ass, trying to pull him deeper with every stroke. "This feels so good."

Jon intended to push her a level or twenty above good. This first time would be spectacular. "Maggie," he murmured between thrusts. "Let me take care of you. Let me get us there."

"Yes. Anything you want."

He gradually slowed, groaning when her channel clamped down, trying to keep his cock inside. He rested the tip just inside the opening to her sex. Despite his thundering heart and the urgency pounding at him, he found that Zen spot and began.

One, two, three, four shallows thrusts, where he only went halfway into her pussy. On the fifth thrust, his cock stayed buried deep. He stayed that way, not moving, for five beats.

Then one, two, three, four shallow thrusts. On the fifth count he pulled out completely. After five breaths, he slowly stroked the tip of his cock up the contour of her mound, stopping at her clit. Then he dragged the wide, blunt head down, separating her pussy lips with his pulsing flesh until he reached the opening to her body.

He began again.

Maggie went wild. Arching against him. Her fingernails digging into his shoulders. Gouging his ass as she fought for a grip on his sweat-coated skin. Her mouth nipping at his neck. Her tongue tracing the edges of the tattoos on his biceps.

Jon kept up the primal pattern until he started to lose count. He said, "Hang on," and rolled upright, keeping their bodies connected as they faced each other. With his knees spread wide, he sat on his heels, holding onto her ass, raising and lowering her body to counter his upward thrusts.

"I'm gonna come again," she wailed.

The almost violent ripples of her orgasm unleashed his.

Hot pulses jettisoned out of his cock with every squeeze of her pussy muscles around his shaft. His mind blanked even as his body erupted and he gasped for breath.

Teeth scraping against his neck brought him out of his sexual stupor.

"I take it back," Maggie panted against his ear. "Everything I said about you not having rhythm."

FOR A BRIEF second when Maggie woke up, she forgot where she was.

Then soft kisses peppered her shoulder. A rough hand on her belly caressed her bare skin. "Mornin', beautiful."

The deep, heavy rasp of Jon's voice was even sexier first thing in the morning. "Mmm. That it is."

"Did you sleep well?"

"When you finally let me sleep." She snuggled her naked body into the warmth of his.

"That didn't sound like a complaint."

"It wasn't."

"Good." Jon's hand slid up to cup her breast. "You want breakfast?"

The rhythmic stroking on her nipple had her arching into his touch and a moan slipped out.

His low-pitched growl drifted into her ear. "That purr is the sexiest thing I've ever heard, so maybe we oughta get out of bed now before we end up spending the whole damn day here."

"I'd like that, except I have to be in Rapid City this afternoon for dance rehearsal." She groaned. "Crap. And after a night like that, I completely forgot that my car is dead."

Jon rolled her over to face him. "I'll call up my mechanic buddy and send him over to look at it. He'll probably need to tow it."

"That's fine. Tell him there's a spare key in a rip in the upholstery underneath the passenger's seat."

"Handy. Now we won't have to leave." His lips glided over hers in a barely there kiss. "Eggs and toast all right?"

"Mmm-hmm." Maggie pressed a kiss to his Adam's apple. "Do you have an extra toothbrush?"

"Bottom right drawer in the guest bath." Jon got up and stretched beside the bed.

Talk about a nice visual first thing in the morning. Perfectly round buns, slim hips widening into a muscular back, defined biceps, triceps and forearms—all wrapped up in that gorgeous tawny skin. Such a shame that he tugged on a pair of long athletic shorts and covered up before he headed to the master bathroom.

Maggie snatched the tank top off the floor on her way to

the guest bath. Maybe she snooped while searching for toothpaste. She didn't find anything that'd lead her to believe he regularly entertained overnight female guests.

Would it have made a difference if you'd found fruit-scented body wash?

No. But she'd be wary if she'd found tampons, makeup or a hair straightener. Those items suggested a permanent, recurring female presence.

After scrubbing her teeth, washing her face and attempting to de-snarl her hair, Maggie padded to the kitchen.

Jon's wide smile made her weak-kneed. "To hell with cookin'. You look good enough to eat."

"I believe you dined on me last night. Twice."

"True. But it didn't fill me up. Only increased my appetite for more." He grabbed a fistful of her hair, angling her head back to plunder her mouth with a thorough kiss.

There was the belly-churning sensation she experienced every time he touched her.

"You're too tempting," he murmured and released her. "You want tomatoes and cheese in your scrambled eggs?"

"Sure. Do you want me to do anything?"

"Just look pretty at my breakfast table while I serve you."

"How much honey did you pour in your coffee this morning, rock star?"

Jon laughed. "None. It's all the gospel truth. Sit."

Maggie sipped strong coffee and watched him multitask, cooking bacon, eggs and toast and slicing fruit. Then he slid a plate in front of her, heaping with food. "Do I look hungry?"

"We burned plenty of calories last night and you'll burn even more dancing today so eat up." He sat across from her with an equally mounded plate.

She shoveled in a bite and swallowed. "These eggs are amazing."

"Thanks. I got to thinking… I'll drive you to Rapid today since you won't have a car. There's stuff I need to do and I can hang around in town until you're done rehearsing. Maybe I'll convince you to have a late dinner with me and breakfast tomorrow morning."

Maggie drained her coffee and got up for a refill, absent-mindedly refilling Jon's cup too.

He placed his hand on her wrist. "Did I say something wrong?"

"No. It's just…" Her eyes searched his. "Why are you with me?"

"I like being with you. I want to get to know you outside the dance studio. And outside the bedroom." His fingers skated up her arm in that seductive way that caused goose flesh to cover her arms. "Although you won't hear me complaining if you wanna get better acquainted there too."

She smooched his smirking mouth. "Fine. I'll accept your

gracious offer, but you've gotta do one thing for me."

"Name it."

"Come out with us tonight. I usually hang out with Seth, his partner Stanis, and Seth's sister Sara after rehearsal."

"Sounds like fun." Jon left the kitchen to call the mechanic.

After Maggie finished loading the dishwasher, she turned to see Jon leaning against the wall. She still did a double take whenever she saw him. The man was stunning with his fiercely beautiful face and his badass posture. It seemed like a dream that she'd had her hands and mouth all over his incredible body last night; and that he'd had that sinful mouth and those talented hands all over her.

Jon was the most enthralling man she'd ever met, but he was difficult to read. There was almost a…"proper" aspect to his personality and mannerisms. Did that stem from him being Native American? Or had the record label's PR agency put all that polish on Johnny Feather over the years? The only glimpse she'd seen of the wild man rock star had been on stage, when he was lost to everything but the music. Although, she had gotten a hint of that intensity last night, when he'd been focused solely on her.

"You're staring at me," he said with amusement.

"You were staring at me first. Besides, you are very easy on the eyes, Jon White Feather."

He kept his arms folded over his chest and continued studying her.

"What? Do I have egg on my face or something?"

"No. Just thinking about how hot last night was. It's taking every damn bit of my willpower not to bend you over the counter and fuck you until you fall apart in my arms again."

There was that animalistic side.

"That thought will keep." Jon inclined his head toward the sliding glass door. "Come on. I've got something to show you."

Maggie looked at the tank top that barely skimmed her hips. "I'm not wearing pants."

"Nobody around besides me to see you. If I had my way? You'd be wearing just that creamy skin."

Oh man. He'd cranked the seduction meter on high today.

He opened the sliding glass door.

Maggie stepped onto a concrete patio and her gaze followed a stone pathway that ended at a large asymmetrical structure. Pine needles, leaves and broken pinecones were scattered across the walkway.

"The storm did some damage." He moved in front of her and bent at the waist. "Climb on."

"Seriously, Jon? A piggyback ride?"

"Yep. You wanted to ride me like a pony. This is kinda close."

How was she supposed to think about anything besides sex with her crotch pressing against his spine, her chest rubbing over the firm muscles of his upper back and her arms draped around his neck?

Maggie released a little whoop and jumped on.

He raced forward. Upon reaching the door, he turned his head. "This is handy. I can spin you around and have my wicked way with you up against the wall."

"Was that what you wanted to show me?"

"Nope."

"Dang. Dash a girl's hopes."

Jon set her on her feet, and all of a sudden seemed hesitant to open the door.

She remembered how much he valued his privacy and suspected he regretted the spontaneous invite into his private domain. "I'd understand if you've changed your mind and don't want me invading your sacred space."

"I want you here." He touched her face. "I once had a teacher who swore no space was truly sacred, except for sexual organs."

"Well, we've already breached each other's sacred spaces. Several times."

Jon laughed and opened the door.

The clean lines and neutral colors utilized feng shui to create a sense of peace and order. A lounging area with deep-cushioned couches was away from the creative heart of the space—the sound-proofed recording area. A window in that room faced out; everything else was closed off. The entire back wall was lined with percussion instruments. Along the outside walls were guitars and cases that held string instruments, woodwinds and brass. She squinted at a table in the corner with an auto-harp and a mandolin. Drums didn't have a place of honor, but were scattered everywhere in sizes and shapes she'd never seen.

"Jon. I'm blown away. What a perfect creative environment. Although I'd be tempted to goof around with all the…omigod, is that a xylophone?"

"Yes, ma'am."

"Do you play it?"

"Sometimes. I used to have to move it to sleep, since I built the studio before the house."

"Because your music matters more to you than anything," she murmured, running her hand over the top of a kettle drum.

His deep voice tickled her ear. "I don't want to say music is my life, but I guess it is because I cannot imagine my life without it."

"No wonder you wanted to stop touring. You have everything you need right here to make music and be happy."

She felt Jon tense behind her. Had she said something wrong? Before she could ask him, he sidestepped her and grabbed a mallet and pounded on the skins, not randomly, but in a rapid-fire pattern that sounded melodic. Who knew drums even had a melody?

Maggie faced him.

Immediately Jon stopped drumming. "What?"

"If it's not too much bother will you play something for me today?"

"Maggie. I'd be honored to play for you." His gaze moved over her as thoroughly as a caress. "Would you dance naked for me while I play?"

"No." She bit her lip. "Well. Maybe. I've never done that before, so it might be fun."

He picked up a maraca and rattled it. "Know what else might be fun? If I recorded you playing something in the background of my drum solo while you're dancing naked."

"No way. I don't play an instrument, not a real one anyway. I don't sing."

"Not even karaoke?"

"Especially not karaoke." She poked him in the chest. "But I'll warn you, I rock at *Rock Band*."

He lifted a brow. "Is that a challenge?"

"Absolutely. Seth, Stanis, Sara and I have a *Rock Band* play-off. I think he mentioned this Saturday night we were gonna shred it." She cocked her head. "But I'm sure you wouldn't be interested. Probably worried you'd get shown up by two gay guys, a nurse and a computer geek."

"You do know that I'm *in* an actual rock band, right?"

"I've heard that doesn't make a difference."

Jon laughed. "Wanna bet?"

Nine

MAGGIE SHOULDN'T HAVE bet against Jon. He ruled at *Rock Band*, destroying all of Seth's previous high scores.

Jon's victory demanded concessions from Maggie— including her spending Saturday night and all day Sunday with him.

She hadn't minded losing at all.

They'd stayed up late Saturday night and stargazed. After-ward they'd rolled around naked in his living room and in his bedroom. After a leisurely breakfast, where they'd lost track of time discussing everything from philosophy to books to movies, they adjourned to his studio.

She dinked around with his computerized sound system while he laid down drum tracks for a mysterious project. Jon was tightlipped when it came to his career—maybe because he feared it was stalled? She didn't sense restlessness in him, so maybe he was content living in one place for more than a night or two. The more they hung out, the more Maggie understood how important it was to him that she saw him as a regular guy, not just Johnny Feather, rocker.

Rather than take Jon's car, Maggie bummed a ride to work from her brother on Monday morning. It seemed odd that she and Billy saw less of each other since she'd relocated to Spearfish from Rapid City. Granted, he had a lot on his mind with a major project he was designing, and a baby on the way, so when he asked about her recent job interviews, she didn't mention the upcoming dance competition. Or Jon.

Maggie raced around town Monday afternoon after she retrieved her car and barely made it to the community center on time for the dance class. Jon was a no show and she checked her disappointment. She'd hoped he would finish out the last week for his niece's benefit, but his absence hadn't bothered Raven. She and her replacement partner, a cute charmer named Thomas Fast Wolf, were enthralled with each other. Enthralled to the point she'd heard Seth quietly threaten to spray the teens down with the fire hose if they didn't quit grinding on each other.

The day off from rehearsing had turned Seth into a task-master. After dance class ended, they performed each competitive rhythm dance fully—the entire thing, not just the focused snippets—three times. Maggie's muscles screamed. The insides of her thighs burned. Her hips were sore.

Maybe that ache wasn't only from dance. Spending the

weekend in bed with Jon had been quite the workout—the man defined insatiable. It'd been an embarrassingly long stretch since Maggie last had a lover, but none of the men she'd been with had that much stamina or sexual creativity. She'd never look at drum tie-down straps the same way again.

The door to the gym banged open. She whirled around and saw Jon. Huh. Usually he was more stealthy than that and she hadn't been sure he'd show up.

His focus remained on her as he strolled across the wooden floor. The tickle in her belly morphed into a full-body tingle when he pulled her into his arms and kissed her.

And kept kissing her. A toe-curling, panty-dampening kiss.

Seth cleared his throat behind them.

Maggie broke the lip lock, but couldn't look away from his heated blue eyes.

Jon grinned. "Hi."

"I like the way you say hi, rock star."

"Thought you might." Jon looked at Seth. "Heya, teach. Is your ass still smarting from me handing it to you this weekend?"

Seth grinned. "I could totally take that the wrong way."

He laughed. "You heading back to Rapid City so I can steal Maggie away now?"

"Yes. I won't miss making that drive after this class ends."

Seth mopped his face and tossed the towel into his duffel bag. "You'll lock up?" he asked Maggie.

"Sure."

"See you tomorrow night, sugar." He smirked at Jon. "Ta to you too, sugar."

Maggie jammed all her belongings into her bag. "I thought maybe you'd come to class tonight."

"I intended to. But this riff wouldn't leave me alone after I dropped you off last night, so I worked on it and didn't go to bed until the sun came up."

"Riff? Isn't that guitar?"

"I play guitar. Having a melody helps me find the right beat."

"Seth will freak out if you kick his ass on *Guitar Hero* too."

Jon gave her that cocky grin again. "He already challenged me and I accepted."

"What were you working on that kept you up all night?"

"I laid down some tracks after I finally got them to sound right. By the time I got up, worked out, and caught up on business stuff, it was too late to come to class."

"Were the tracks for any project in particular?"

He shrugged and snagged her bag, draping the strap over his shoulder. "Nothin' I can talk about."

"Or don't wanna talk about. Still, it's gotta be a relief to work without pressure. Not having to worry about wrapping up an idea too fast because you've gotta get back on the road or meet some record label deadline."

"If only it were that easy."

Sometimes the man was so damn cryptic.

As Maggie locked the door she couldn't help but yawn.

"It appears my timing is still off." Jon swept his thumb under her eye. "You're exhausted, dancing queen."

She bristled. "I know I look like shit, but I worked eight hours today and danced for five—"

Jon smothered her protest with his mouth, gifting her with a kiss that had her melting against him. He slid his lips down her chin and nibbled beneath her jawline, knowing it drove her crazy. "I only meant you're too tired for what I had in mind tonight."

"Which was what? Crazy wild monkey sex hanging from a tree?"

"No. A candlelight dinner and…"

"And…what? Because you seem awful disappointed I'm dragging ass."

"I hadn't gotten further than that, except hoping we'd get in wild-monkey-sex naked-time afterward, which ain't exactly romantic to admit before I've wined and dined you. But right now I'm leaning toward just tucking you straight in bed."

Maggie tipped her head back to gaze at him. When she wore flat shoes Jon was eight inches taller than her five foot five. "You're sending me to bed without supper? Was I bad or something?"

"No. You're good. Very, very good." Jon teased her lips with deceptively gentle kisses that packed an erotic punch. "That's the problem. I can't stop thinking about you, Maggie."

"I know. I thought we'd figured this out over the weekend when we both said we wanted to see where this goes…and it seems like we're going in opposite directions with opposite schedules."

"Well, then, we'll have to learn to compromise." Jon crowded her against the brick wall, bracing his hands beside her head. "You have to eat, right? Some days we can meet for lunch."

She twined her arms around his neck. "And some nights we'll have a late supper."

"Some mornings, we'll have breakfast in bed." He nuzzled her temple. "Selfish of me to hope that's most mornings?"

"Then that'd make me selfish too, because I have the same wish." Maggie had a moment of panic after the words tumbled out. She never put herself out there so fast. She always held part of herself back in a relationship, especially early on, not wanting to appear overeager or act desperate.

He peered into her eyes. "What just happened? You tensed up."

"Nothing."

"Bull. Talk to me."

"I've never known another man like you. Not personally. I've watched hot guys like you from afar, in class, or on stage, or on TV, but I haven't ever been the lucky one who gets to make time with the gorgeous man all the other women want."

"Make time?" he repeated. "You think that's all I'm doing? I lured you into my bed because I was bored? I'm killing time with you until someone better comes along?"

"Or until you get bored and leave town."

His mouth tightened.

"I know it's my insecurity, but I can't pretend I've been in this position before."

"What position is that?"

Maggie ran her fingers down his face. "Scared. Wanting those breakfasts in bed. Wanting to believe every sweet, raunchy word you say to me."

"Then take a leap of faith and believe it," he said softly.

"That's the thing about leaps of faith; I'm not so good at taking them because I tend to fall flat on my face."

"Then let's take it together, because I've never been in this position either."

She found that hard to believe. "Really?"

"Yes. I haven't stuck around here long enough to get to know a woman on any level besides sexual. And it wouldn't matter anyway because I've never been with a woman like you,

Maggie. You're classy. And smart. And generous with your time. You're patient. And so damn sweet it makes me ache." His eyes took on a glint of pure male animal. "Then I watch you dance and I almost can't breathe. The way you move is the sexiest thing I've ever seen. It's passion and poetry."

She couldn't be more stunned. "Jon—"

"Let me finish. Being with you is starting to strip the barriers I've had up for years. Because even though you do see me as the guy who's a hit with the ladies, that's not all you see. You treat me as Jon, not Johnny. You make me laugh. You make me think. It's not all about sex with you. Yet, you make me so fucking hot that I want to slide up in you, right here, right now, just to see that dreamy look you get when I'm inside you." He rested his forehead to hers. "So yeah, this is beyond my realm of experience. But I'm not scared by it because it feels so damn right." He paused and murmured, "Am I wrong?"

"No." She kissed him then. Not with tenderness, but an openmouthed explosion of need, showing him his faith in her—in this, in what was building between them—wasn't misplaced.

By the time they broke apart, her panties were wet, her nipples hard, her head was buzzing and she seriously considered ripping his clothes off with her teeth.

"Come home with me," she panted against his throat.

"And we'll get started on that breakfast thing."

TUESDAY NIGHT AFTER Maggie's dance rehearsal, Jon picked her up for a romantic moonlight stroll by the creek.

Wednesday they indulged in a long lunch, picnic style, in Jon's bed.

Thursday Jon snuck into the gym for the last night of dance class. Staying in the shadows, he watched his niece move with more confidence, shyly flirting with the too-charming Fast Wolf boy, who should've been named Fast Hands. Lurking gave him a feeling of disconnection and he left without letting anyone know he'd even been there.

His melancholy mood didn't go to waste; he channeled it into his music. He'd been inspired to write more than usual in the past week. So when his agent called, Jon mentioned his recent increased output and that he'd already passed the audio files to Push, Radioactive Tar and Darkly Dreaming. But Marty also wanted to know if Johnny intended to enter into serious negotiations with any of the three bands.

That was the crux of Jon's problem; although the music-career fairy had knocked, he wasn't sure which door to open—if any. When his Sapa bandmate Jeps had called a few hours later to discuss the future of the band, Jon hedged. He loved and respected his Sapa bandmates, yet, he'd experienced an unprecedented burst of creativity in the last month and he was damn proud of the work he'd finished.

He wondered how much of it was due to breaking away from Sapa. Maybe when he wasn't collaborating with other musicians he had a clearer vision of his own musical style. Maybe the possibility of working with the most respected producers in the business forced him to step up his game. Maybe being settled at home for an extended period of time allowed his creativity to flow more freely.

Or maybe he could attribute it all to being around Maggie and truly being happy.

Friday night he whisked her back to his place after her rehearsal with Seth. Filled with excess energy, Maggie jumped him, riding him to an orgasm so intense he had rug burns on his ass and he'd momentarily lost the ability to speak.

Since the dance competition was a mere week away, Seth had scheduled an all-weekend rehearsal. Jon knew if he began a new project he'd obsess until he finished it, so he opted to drop by Jim's house on Saturday instead of working. He riled up the kids, drank a beer and pretended he wasn't counting down the hours until he saw Maggie.

He loved surprising her so he'd rented a room at a secluded bed and breakfast and arranged the candlelight dinner he'd promised her. After returning to the room, Jon massaged her sore muscles and made love to her in the big Jacuzzi tub and the enormous four-poster bed. It was one of the best weekends of his life—the perfect mix of work and play, family, romance, passion, fun and relaxation.

So it was bittersweet when Marty called him and insisted he get to L.A. for meetings on Monday. He knew the meetings wouldn't be limited to California, and he resigned himself to being gone another week. But since all of this was preliminary, he couldn't discuss the particulars with Maggie or anyone else.

Normally Jon waited outside in the parking lot of the dance studio for Maggie to finish because Seth insisted on closed rehearsals. But he didn't have a lot of time so Seth could overlook the interruption just once since Jon was leaving town.

The entryway of the small studio was a dancer's ready room, comprised of lockers, wall pegs, bins and benches. The largest wall was also a window; observation glass on one side and a mirror on the other.

Even with the door to the studio closed, Jon could hear Seth and Maggie yelling at each other.

Whoa. He'd never seen Maggie so angry.

"I cannot do it like that, Seth. I've told you ten times. It won't work. I haven't done that technique in years and I'm not about to add it into the routine less than a week before competition!"

Seth got right in her face. "That's a load of crap, Maggie.

You don't want to do it just because it's hard. You'd rather make the easy move and you know what? It'll make you look lazy. And make me look lazy, because not only am I your partner, I'm your dance coach."

"Lazy?" Maggie repeated. She shoved Seth back a step. "Fuck off. I've busted my ass and I haven't taken the easy way out on anything. You're just afraid no one will take you seriously as a choreographer if you don't put some stupid, worthless fancy-ass dance move in just to show you know how to do it."

"That was a bitchy thing to say."

"It's the truth. And you're being an asshole about it."

"Tough shit. You will do what I say. Period. End of discussion." Seth stomped off, grabbed the remote and turned the music back on.

Maggie didn't budge.

A door opened and Seth's partner, Stanis, exited the office. But he didn't offer his usual flirtatious smile.

"They still snapping at each other?" he asked Jon.

"Yeah. How long has it been going on?"

"An hour. And before you ask why I didn't put a stop to it, I'll remind you of my 'no interference' policy."

Jon lifted a brow. "So you're good with them verbally assaulting each other? Or do you step in only when it turns physical?"

Stanis smoothed his fingers down his silk tie. "It won't ever get to that point."

A loud crash sounded and Jon spun around to see Maggie sprawled on the floor with Seth yelling at her to quit being such a baby and get back up and do it again.

Jon stormed into the studio, stepping between Maggie and Seth. When he glanced down and saw Maggie's face wet with tears, it took every ounce of restraint not to knock Seth on his ass. Jon plucked her off the floor and set her on a bench.

Seth shouted, "What do you think you're doing? This is a closed rehearsal and you have no right to barge in here—"

He was looming over Seth in two seconds. "I have every right when I see Maggie on the floor! What the fuck is wrong with you, Seth? I know you're her coach, but I didn't think you were a bully. It's obvious she's had enough if she's crying."

That seemed to knock the fight right out of Seth.

Stanis wrapped his arm around Seth's shoulder. "Jon is right, sweetheart. Take a break. Come on." He led Seth out of the studio and the office door closed.

Jon forced deep breaths into his lungs before he faced Maggie.

She'd stopped crying, but she still looked miserable.

"You all right?"

She shook her head and tears spilled down her cheeks.

He scooped her onto his lap, running his hands down her

spine as her body was racked with sobs. "Ssh. Baby. It's okay."

"I hate him," she said with a hiccup.

"No, you don't. You're both on edge and you've spent way too much time together."

"I want to quit."

Jon pressed his lips against her forehead. "No, you don't."

A few minutes passed before she said, "But I could. The company in Billings I sent my resume to after I was laid off has an opening. They want to interview me this week."

"Which is great. But Maggie, you shouldn't be making any career decisions before your first major dance competition."

"Maybe I should take it as a sign that I should quit."

"You'd be kicking yourself if you didn't follow through with competing in regionals after all the work you've put into it the last six months."

"You're probably right. Anyway. Why are you here?"

"To tell you I have to deal with some business out of town."

She lifted her head. "You're leaving again?"

He smoothed damp tendrils of hair from her face. "Yeah."

"I thought Sapa was on an extended break and you were taking time off?"

Jon hated sidestepping the issue, but Maggie had enough stress in her life this week. And he was scared she'd just walk away if he told her the truth. "It's just...I didn't want to leave without saying goodbye this time."

"Thanks for that." She sighed. "It's probably for the best that you'll be gone."

"Since I won't see you anyway because of your intensive rehearsal schedule?"

"Partially. But also because of this." Maggie angled her head so he could see the large hickey on her neck.

"Shit. Sorry about that."

"No, you're not. I'm not either, because last night was incredible." She pressed her lips to his. "But I will say Seth wasn't happy about the obvious suck marks on my neck and chest. He warned me that if you continued to act like a horny teen then he wouldn't allow me to see you at all this week."

Jon whistled. "Is he grounding you from TV and your car too?"

"And he's taking away my allowance and my cell phone."

He couldn't help but grin that she'd retained her sense of humor even under duress.

"As you can probably guess, his threat didn't go over very well. The day started off on the wrong foot and went downhill from there."

"So you're doubly happy I bulled my way in and told him off?" he asked dryly.

"Yes. Because no one ever sticks up for me." Maggie rested her cheek against the curve of his neck. "But I am going to miss you."

"Same here." Jon adjusted her position so she faced him with her knees on either side of his thighs. He framed her face in his hands and devoured her with a drawn-out kiss that wasn't nearly enough. "Don't overdo it this week, dancing queen."

"I won't. Don't sweat it if you can't make it back for the competition on Saturday."

He locked his gaze to hers. "I'll be there."

"But—"

"No buts. I'll be there. I promise."

Ten

"STOP FIDGETING."

Maggie gave Seth a cool look. "Gimme a break. I haven't competed in years. I'm entitled to fidgeting. And pacing. And pure panic."

Seth curled his hands around her shoulders. "Listen to me. We are on top of the world, baby. We make a fabulous team. Some dancers are already asking who we are. We're the sandbaggers, Maggie."

She blinked at him. "Isn't that a given? Since we're unknown?"

"It's a head game. I saw you eyeing the others' costumes. Yes, they are much better than ours." Seth dropped his voice. "Sweetie. That's intentional. I can get my hands on top-of-the-line costumes, but why overplay our hand? Better to underplay it and have our competitors dismiss us as country bumpkins trying to dance in the big leagues."

"I see your point."

"These dancers have sponsors. We don't. Luckily for us, that means when we win this competition, we'll be attractive to sponsors because no one has heard of us. And the sponsors will look smart for snapping up an up-and-coming dance team."

Sponsorship was almost too much to hope for. "Not to put the cart before the horse, but say we win. We score sponsors. Then what happens?"

Seth adjusted the seams on her sleeves. "Then we have the means to hit more competitions, notch more wins, which will get us invited to dance in exhibition showcases and we both know that's where the real money is. Plus, we build name recognition while we're doing it. And fingers crossed…" He paused a beat too long before he stepped back. "Never mind."

Her stomach lurched at his vague tone. "What?"

"I've been hesitant to tell you this before now, because I knew it'd freak you out. But if we win, Vladimir Konski has agreed to audition us for possible coaching for nationals."

"Seriously? He's huge. He coached… Well, obviously I don't have to tell you who he coached." Maggie narrowed her eyes. "Hey. How did you manage that?"

Seth winked. "I dated Vladimir's son Niko when we were in *The Will Rogers Follies* in New York. Niko and I've stayed on good terms and he might've mentioned to his father that I'm dipping my toe into the competitive dance waters."

Pumped up by the possibilities, she gave him a smacking kiss on the mouth. "Let's show them how it's done, partner."

Maggie's butterflies didn't settle as she checked her makeup. Her hair. Her costume. Her shoes. She glanced at Seth, performing the same rituals.

Then they were in the chute, waiting for their number to be called. They didn't speak to anyone, nor did they chat with each other. She mentally reviewed the steps for the first dance.

Finally they heard, "Dancers in position."

Seth smiled, snatched her hand and then it was game on.

Now they just had to get through the next ten minutes, dance their asses off and blow the other eleven couples out of the water.

At the start of the music, Maggie became someone else. She and Seth circled each other. Not as dance partners, not as friends, but as potential sexual conquests, turning up the heat as they set their bodies in motion.

The first dance was the cha-cha, flirty and fun as she made promises with her eyes and her hips. During the second dance, the rhumba, she morphed into the seductress, using sensual moves to entice her potential lover. The third dance was swing, a hopping, energetic show of stamina and athleticism. The fourth dance, the bolero, was filled with passion and longing as their bodies undulated in unison and opposition. And the fifth dance, the mambo, was back to a sexy tease.

She and Seth were in perfect synch throughout all five dances. They maintained the intensity even during the thirty-second pause between each ninety-second piece of music.

After they finished dancing, Maggie's body pulsed with sexual energy and adrenaline. Waiting for the results was excruciating, but at least they were expected to leave the dance floor while the judges made their decision.

Seth clasped her hand as they dodged other dancers, who were also pumped after their performances.

By the time they reached the corner they'd staked out in the dressing area, the *touch me, fuck me, take me now* vibe between them had cooled.

Or so she thought.

Seth handed her a bottle of grape-flavored Gatorade and took one for himself, staring at her with an expression she'd never seen directed at her.

Maggie wondered if there'd be awkward moments in the aftermath of suggestive dancing. She'd become sexually involved with her dance partner in college, so this situation wasn't uncharted territory for her, but Seth was gay.

Then Seth allowed her a wolfish grin. "My God, woman, if I was straight I'd be fucking you balls deep against that wall right now. Which tells me our performance was off the charts."

That had been the perfect thing to say. She grinned. "It just proves that having the steps drilled into my head works best because I could concentrate on the presentation, not the choreography."

Seth nodded. "I don't want to ruin this beautiful high by dissecting our performance. I want to bask in my foresight for choosing such an excellent dancing partner." He toasted her with his plastic bottle.

Maggie blushed from his praise. "I'm grateful you believed there was potential in me."

"There's better than potential, baby, there's heat between us on the floor. I'll bet Stanis is fit to be tied after our sexy presentation." Seth drained his Gatorade. "I imagine bad-boy rocker came to support you?"

"Of course he knows about it, but…"

"But what?"

She hadn't heard from Jon at all the last five days. "I'm not sure if he's back in town. And I don't want to pressure him to support me because we're keeping this casual."

"I've seen how that man looks at you, Maggie, and there's nothing casual about it. Johnny-hottie is completely smitten with you," Seth continued. "So don't assume he's only interested in playing a little grab-ass with you before he moves on."

"I wish I could believe that."

Seth gave her a thoughtful look. "Maybe this will convince

you. Do you remember the last week of dance class when newlywed Ashley popped into the gym on Friday night, wearing tiny booty shorts and her tight sports bra that showed off her gigantic fake boobs?"

Confused, Maggie squinted at him. "I was there? I don't remember."

Seth pointed at her. "Exactly. You were engrossed in working with the scarves for perfecting movement flow. Johnny-hottie didn't pay attention to Ashley at all; he was absolutely mesmerized by you."

Her mouth dropped open. "Jon was at our rehearsal?"

"I'm pretty sure he'd been lifting weights, because his muscles were all bulgy and he was covered in a delicious sheen of sweat." Seth laughed when Maggie's eyes widened. "What? I can look. Not that he noticed me ogling him since he only had eyes for you."

"Ladies and gentleman, we have our winners," boomed over the loudspeakers.

"This is it." Seth took her hand and dragged her out of the dressing area and into the arena.

Her gut clenched. Her heart raced. But she plastered on a smile as they lined up on the dance floor.

The committee chair went on about each judge before announcing their decisions in the top three slots.

Third place was announced and it wasn't them.

Second place was announced and it wasn't them.

A drum roll sounded. "The winners of the American Dance Federation Rhythm Style competition, who will represent the Mountain States region at the National Finals in Orlando, are…"

And their names were announced.

Maggie was pretty sure her feet didn't touch the floor as she and Seth performed a sweeping bow and deep curtsey to the crowd before they floated to the judge's stand to accept the medals, the check and flowers.

Other dancers surrounded them to offer congratulations— a few remarks were even genuine.

After the floor cleared, Maggie spun around, her gaze searching the stands.

Then she saw Jon. The intense way he looked at her put her feet in motion and she tried really hard not to skip.

Jon dangled over the railing so far Maggie thought he might fall. And that grin. Boy howdy it made her all tingly.

"You came." Brilliant observation, Maggie.

"I told you I'd be here. That was the most amazing dance performance I've ever seen."

"Man, you guys totally rocked it!" Raven gushed. "You were so much better than everyone else. It was obvious after the first dance that you and Seth were gonna win."

Her focus on Jon had been so absolute she hadn't noticed

Raven. She smiled at her. "I'm glad you came. It was nice of your uncle to bring you."

Then Seth bounded over. "If it isn't my two favorite students!"

Raven started chattering to Seth and Maggie glanced at Jon. He stepped sideways, motioning for a word in private. "You look beautiful."

"Thank you." She noticed he held a single white rose with pink-tipped petals. "Is that for me?"

"Yeah. Makes me look cheap, compared to those." Jon pointed to the bouquet of a dozen red roses in her arms.

"These weren't bought specifically for me, like your rose was. So gimme."

He laughed. "I was told this color is called minuet, so I thought you'd appreciate that." He bent down until they were eye to eye. "But the real reason I bought it is because the pink on cream tones reminded me of the color of your skin after you've come undone in my arms."

The rough rasp of his voice sent sexual heat surging through her.

"You're ramped up right now," he half growled. "I can feel it. Baby, it's pulsing off you."

She turned her head, letting her lips graze the corner of his mouth. "I'd like to drag you off and put this excess energy to good use."

"Let's go. Right now."

His warm breath teased her ear and she wanted to feel his whispers drifting over every inch of her skin.

"Maggie?"

Seth's voice pulled her out of the moment, forcing her to step back from the magnetic hold Jon had on her. "Ah. What?"

"A couple of potential sponsors want to talk to us and we shouldn't keep them waiting."

"Go on," Jon urged. "I'll catch up with you later."

Maggie gave him a promising smile and dashed away with Seth.

FOUR HOURS LATER, Maggie stood on the front porch of her cabin. The day had been a scorcher and the sudden rainstorm caused steam to rise from the pavement like ghostly fingers.

Leaning against the railing, she listened to the steady din on the tin roof as raindrops splashed her bare feet. The humid air smelled clean, heavy with the earthy scent of soil and vegetation.

What a whirlwind week. In addition to hours of rehearsal, she'd decided to meet with that rep from the consulting company based out of Billings. He hadn't offered her a job, but the interview had gone well enough she suspected an offer would be coming in the next few weeks.

Would she take it? In the last six months she'd enjoyed having a job and not the pressure of a career. As much as she loved dancing, she didn't want it to become another obligation she'd resent. But now with this win, she was in limbo for two more months.

The meetings with potential sponsors had gone better than expected. Evidently word had spread of their couples dance classes at the community center. The owners of a travel agency, big supporters of the arts, offered to sponsor all their airfare expenses for preparation for the national competition in Florida.

Seth had spent the drive back to Spearfish on the phone with Vladimir, setting up an audition in Salt Lake City next weekend and a backup audition with another teacher in Dallas. Maggie could swing the price of hotel and food costs, but those were a drop in the bucket compared to Vladimir's fees for private instruction. How would she pay for them?

She'd cross that bridge when she came to it.

Speaking of crossing the bridge…headlights bumped up the drive and Jon's Land Cruiser pulled into view.

Anticipation rolled through her. She'd missed him more than she thought possible in the last week, not just the sex but talking to him. Jon was a great listener—not a trait she expected from a man used to having people fawning over him. His stories about life on the road entertained her, but also indicated how hard he'd worked to grow his career and showed his joy at the connection he'd built with his fans. He had her laughing whenever he talked about his family and growing up on the reservation. Jon White Feather was a sweet, funny, thoughtful man who didn't let his onstage persona define him offstage.

And Maggie was falling for him so fast it scared her.

Jon climbed out and sauntered toward her. His hot, sensual gaze traveled from her eyes to her mouth, lingering on her chest and then meandering back up to her eyes.

Maggie felt that erotic caress as if his hands were already on her. No denying a large part of their attraction was purely physical. So while she appreciated all the other great traits Jon had, right now, she wanted to gorge herself on the sexual side of him.

She jumped the two stairs and raced toward him, her feet sinking into ankle-deep mud.

Jon met her halfway, catching her when she launched herself at him. Their lips connected, the openmouthed kiss a ravenous explosion of passion and need.

Maggie clutched his neck, then her hands moved down his muscled biceps, dragging him closer as his fingers twined in her hair.

He groaned and broke the kiss, his hot mouth following the arc of her neck. "Maggie. God." He nipped at the section of skin where her neck met her shoulder. "I couldn't take my eyes off you today. You had me under your spell. You owned me."

Maggie dropped her head back, allowing him access to the other side of her neck. She was so lost in the total seduction of his mouth on her skin that she barely noticed the raindrops on her face.

His hips rocked forward, driving her toward the steps.

Her toes were cooled by the spongy wet grass, but her body was on fire, craving his deft touch. "I want you," she whispered against his mouth. "Now. My way."

"Yes. You've got me."

Her fingertips raked his chest as her mouth continued its southerly progression. Palming his hips, Maggie dropped to her knees and dragged his athletic shorts to his ankles.

How lucky that Jon had gone commando.

"Maggie. Baby. You don't—"

"Shut up and lose the shirt."

When the soaking wet cotton fabric was gone, she had access to his gloriously hard, wonderfully long cock. Maggie's hands followed the outside of his lower half, from his ridged calves to his knees, and across those strong quads. She nuzzled his groin, breathing him in.

Jon tugged on the stretchy strap of her camisole. "Fair's fair, dancing queen. I wanna feel your skin against mine."

Maggie yanked off her top. Although the night was dark,

the light from the window reflected off his face and body. Rain drizzled down his torso, highlighting the dips and valleys of his incredible musculature. He was magnificent naked, even more magnificent naked and wet.

She brushed a kiss over the sun tattoo below his left hip and the moon tat mirrored on the right side. His belly quivered beneath her lips. Tilting her head back, she locked her gaze to his as she sucked his shaft deeply into her mouth.

"Ah. Dammit. That's so…" He moaned. His legs were rigid and he maintained a firm grip on her head.

She reveled in the power of rendering him speechless. Her fingers formed a circle at the base of his shaft and she stroked up while her mouth and tongue worked him from the cockhead down.

Each bob of her head made her as wet on the inside as she was on the outside.

He'd never let her go this far before, always pulling out before he finished in her mouth. But this time she wanted to feel the pulses on her tongue as he spilled his seed. She wanted him to feel her throat working as she swallowed every spurt.

"You're killing me," he panted. "Stop."

She shook her head vehemently and clamped his tight butt cheek in her left hand, holding him in place.

"I…" was all he managed, along with a deep groan as he erupted, warm and wet, against her tongue.

Her mouth formed a seal around his dick as she sucked down every drop. His cock remained hard even after he'd been spent completely. She continued to suck and nuzzle him, aching for relief from the sticky heat that throbbed between her thighs.

Then Jon's fingers curled over her jawline to lift her chin. His thumbs traced her cheekbones. He didn't say a word—he didn't have to—everything he felt was right there in his eyes.

Rain still fell. Not in a torrential downpour, but soft drops.

Maggie might've been cold if not for the inferno burning inside her.

Jon recognized that fire—that primal need—and pounced, pushing her onto the grass. He followed her down, making short work of her shorts. His hands spread her thighs apart and he buried his face in her pussy.

She gasped at the shock of his cold cheeks and lips against her hot tissue. Then his warm tongue lapped the juices coating her sex. He licked her slit, a growl vibrating as he suckled her pussy lips.

"I fucking love how wet you are after you blow me." His hands slid beneath her buttocks and he raised her hips, burrowing his tongue more deeply inside her channel.

This time there was no finesse to his oral hunger. He took after her like a starving man. A long lick, a tongue thrust, a deliberate graze of his teeth. Not teasing her, but feasting on her slick, sensitive flesh until he'd had his fill.

So when his mouth settled over her clit, all it took was four hard sucks and she climaxed. Hard. Thrashing beneath him, throwing water everywhere, but he held her tightly through each intense wave.

A loud clap of thunder forced her from the deep well of pleasure. She opened her eyes and looked down her body to where Jon's beautiful face rested on her stomach.

He slowly raised his head. And holy shit, the primal look in his eyes stole her breath. He pushed back to his knees, his hand dropping to his groin. He rolled on a condom and stroked his erection. "Turn over."

That rough demand sent a fresh onslaught of heat through her. But something in his posture encouraged her to push him a little further, daring him to give in to that animalistic side completely. So she balanced on her hands and scooted backward, away from him.

"Maggie."

A warning—which she didn't heed. She tossed her wet hair over her shoulder and moved back. "What?"

"I said: Don't. Move."

The wet grass squished between her fingers and toes as she kept moving backward.

Then Jon was on all fours, inching toward her with a lethal sexiness that made her heart race and her sex clench. "You think I won't chase you?"

"I'm counting on you chasing me," she tossed back.

He growled and kicked up the pace.

She tried to crab crawl faster, but Jon was already on her. Water and mud splashed as he flipped her onto her hands and knees, caging her body beneath his.

Her body shook. Not from cold. Not from fear. From this explosion of feelings he forced to the surface. He wanted her. All of her. Without questions or limitations.

His hand was in her hair, pulling her head up and holding it in place. His breath was hot on her neck. "You want me to fuck you like this, Maggie? Down and dirty?" He sank his teeth into the curve of her shoulder, directly on the spot that made her unravel.

She whimpered and bucked against him, but he had her locked down tight.

"Yes or no?"

"Yes. Damn you. Yes. Do it. Do it now."

Jon plundered her mouth with a brutal kiss as he reached between them to drag the wet rim of his cockhead from her clit down to her opening. A brief, breathless pause and then he rammed that hard shaft all the way in.

She gasped at the edgy spike of need. She waited, desperate for another forceful thrust.

But he didn't move. His voice rumbled in her ear. "Can

you hear those rhythms? The driving sound of the rain. The crashing thunder in the sky. The soft ping of tiny water droplets on the roof."

"Jon. Please."

"Hear it. Feel it. But focus only on this. My heartbeat. Yours. Our blood pumping fast and hard. Our bodies so connected that's all there is in this moment."

Maggie almost came right then.

Jon pulled out and slammed back in.

Each thrust was a tiny orgasm, sending chills up and down her spine. She was attuned to him on a deeper level than she'd ever thought possible. The rapid exhalations of his breath on her neck. The muscles in his biceps bunching against her arms. The upward roll of his hips. The sting of his skin slapping into hers. The ground digging into her palms and her knees as he fucked her into oblivion.

"Come for me, Maggie." He pounded into her flesh. "Scream for me."

His hot mouth connected with her rain-cooled skin. He used the rhythm of their bodies to drive her to that soaring crescendo—a peak that Jon held her to until his own cadence synched with hers. Then they rode that long, final pulsing beat together, tumbling end over end into the abyss.

After the white noise stopped roaring in her head, Maggie lifted her face, blinking away the rain to gasp for breath. The swirling mist made her wonder if she was dreaming.

But Jon's molten body moved off hers and his cock slid out in a rush of moisture.

Her arms gave out and she slid gracelessly to the ground. Into the mud. But she didn't care.

He rolled her over and kissed her. And kept kissing her with such fierceness and tenderness, she forgot they were naked outside on the lawn in a rainstorm. Until she started to shiver.

"I know, baby. I'll warm you up."

He lifted her into his arms and carried her inside.

Eleven

THE NEXT MORNING, Jon said, "There's this family thing I have to go to today."

"I'm sure the bridge is passable after last night's rainstorm if you need to leave."

Jon ran his fingertips across the indentations in her lower spine, teasing the fine blond hairs with every pass. "I wasn't trying to skip out on you. I want you to come with me."

She lifted her head and looked at him. "Really?"

"Uh-huh." He kissed her shoulder. "Unless you don't want to."

"It's not that. It's just…" Her eyes searched his. "You're taking me to your family thing?"

"Yes, because my family is important to me. And you're important to me. I would've asked you last night, but I didn't want you to think the afterglow of mind-blowing sex was the reason for the invite."

Maggie rolled flat on her back and smirked. "Speaking of

mind-blowing sex…maybe you should use that sugar-coated mouth of yours to convince me."

"You know I live for a challenge, woman."

AND BECAUSE HE'D risen to the challenge—twice—they were late to the party.

"Are you sure we aren't supposed to bring something?" Maggie asked as they headed up the driveway.

"Nah. My mom and Cindy have it planned down to coordinating plates and napkins."

When Maggie fidgeted with the straps on her sundress, he snagged her hand and kissed her knuckles. "Relax. You look gorgeous. They're gonna love you." *Like I'm starting to.*

Rather than traipsing through the house, Jon led her over the brick walkway to the backyard. Two white canopies had been set up. Food under one, tables under the other. Kids ran everywhere and for once he wasn't mauled the instant he walked in.

He headed toward where his father and brothers—Jim and Jared—were hanging out on the patio.

"Hey, Pops," Jon said, clapping him on the back.

"Good to see you, son." His father focused on Maggie. "You've brought a beautiful guest to our family gathering, eh?"

"Yep. Maggie Buchanan, this is my father, Lyle White

Feather."

"Nice to meet you," Maggie said.

"How do you know our Jon?"

Raven butted in. "She's the dance instructor for the dance class Uncle Jon and I are taking." She lightly punched Jon's arm. "Or were taking. Since *some* of us skipped out and didn't finish the class."

"That means I'll have to take private lessons to catch up. Besides, I heard your new partner Thomas is great at slow dancing," he teased.

Raven blushed.

Jim said, "Great to see you again, Maggie. I keep hoping you'll stop into the office and give that brother of yours grief."

"I would, but Eden claims that's her job and she scares me with all those crazy pregnancy hormones."

Jared stepped forward. "Hey, big bro. Ain't you gonna introduce me to your pretty lady?"

"No."

Then Jared, that buff bastard, laughed and jerked Maggie into a tight hug. "Welcome to the powwow. I'm Jared. The rock star's younger, better-looking, more charming brother."

Jon placed his hands on Maggie's hips and pulled her back, flashing his teeth at Jared. "Find your own woman, she's mine."

Maggie went motionless. She turned her head and looked

up at him.

He kissed her surprised mouth. "What?"

"Do you want me to move so you have room to beat on your chest too?"

Both his brothers and his dad laughed.

"What's so funny, boys?"

Jon faced his mother. "They're picking on me."

"Poor baby." She gave Jon a hug and bussed his cheek, but her focus was on the woman at his side. "You must be Maggie. I'm Jon's mother, MaryAnn. My son has said good things about you."

"I've said good things too, *Unci*," Raven inserted. "You should've seen her and her partner Seth dance at the competition yesterday. They were spectacular."

Maggie grinned. "I wouldn't go that far, Raven, but we were good enough to win."

"Jon, dear, why don't you get Maggie a glass of punch?"

Meaning, take off so I can grill this girl without you hovering.

No way would he subject Maggie to the green goo known as his mother's lime sherbet and pineapple juice punch. He opted to just leave, detouring to the driveway where his nephews were playing basketball.

Among the motley crew of players was Jared's fellow firefighter and best pal, Gabe. "I see my brother dragged you along again."

"Jared needs a keeper."

"No doubt. He suckers you in every time."

"I don't mind." Gabe was always quiet—the opposite of Jared—and Jon wasn't sure how the guys ended up staying roommates for so long.

"Uncle Jon is on our team," Garth crowed.

The score was tied when lunch was announced.

Jon tracked down Maggie, who had been cornered by the twins and looked a little frazzled. Heaven knew his large, loud family could overwhelm him sometimes.

After a gigantic meal, the guys were tasked with cleanup duties. When Jon came back from hauling out the trash, that sneaky bastard Jared had taken the seat next to Maggie and they already appeared to be in deep conversation.

Jon pulled up another chair on Maggie's other side.

"Do you think you would've scored sponsors even if you hadn't won yesterday?" Jared asked Maggie.

She shrugged. "I'm just glad local businesses want to support us." She went on to talk about fostering community involvement in the arts, the great response to dance classes and the request to teach more.

Jared said, "I don't know how you'll be able to teach any new classes if you'll be gone every weekend training until nationals."

That was a new development—and it didn't make Jon happy. "You didn't tell me that you'd be training out of town." Then again, they hadn't done much talking last night. Or this morning.

"Didn't make sense to mention it until it was a done deal. Seth is working out the details. Since there aren't qualified teachers around here, we'll have to go out of state to train."

"How long until nationals?"

"Two months. Which isn't much time to learn a new routine."

Jon frowned. "You'll be gone every weekend for two months? Can't you just use the routine you won with?"

Maggie shook her head. "Whole different playing field, so we have to step up our game. We won't know if we'll be training in Salt Lake or Dallas until mid-next week anyway. If we bomb the auditions this weekend, then we're back to square one finding an instructor on short notice."

"Wait. You're flying to Salt Lake *and* Dallas this weekend?"

"Yes. We leave early Friday morning."

Talk about being left in the dark. "Why didn't I know any of this?"

She fiddled with the hem on her sundress. "Because you were gone last week." *And I didn't hear from you* wasn't said but it sure as hell was implied. "I also had a job interview with the Billings firm on Wednesday." Maggie finally looked at him. "And it went well."

"But I thought you weren't going to add that stress to your week."

"I had to prepare for the possibility we might lose. Our rehearsal schedule will get more intensive. Winning a regional championship was the first leg of the race. Now we're training for a marathon."

Jared leaned over and patted Jon's leg. "Sorry, bro. How much does that suck?"

"What?" he practically snarled.

"You decide to settle down at home after years of nonstop touring and the first woman you hook up with will be on the road as much as you used to be. Is that karma? Or irony?"

Silence.

Maggie stood abruptly. "Excuse me." She took off before Jon could stop her.

"Jesus, Jared, way to be an ass," Gabe said.

Jon pushed to his feet and glared at his brother. "Hook up? Really Jared? Maggie isn't just a hook up for me and you damn well know it."

"That's not what I meant." Jared pleaded with Gabe. "You know what I meant, right?"

Gabe shook his head.

Jared tipped his head back and stared at the sky. "I'm sorry. It's just…you don't drag every woman you're seeing home to meet the family, so I know Maggie is different…Christ. I should keep my damn mouth shut."

"Good plan."

Jon hadn't seen which direction Maggie had gone. He ducked around the side of the house and caught his mother sneaking a cigarette behind the garage. "Hey, cheater. I thought you quit."

"Nope. I'm down to four a day, which is pretty good." She blew out a stream of smoke. "You like this Maggie."

That was a major understatement. "Yep."

"You've been dating what? A couple months? And you're already bringing her to meet us? That's fast for you."

"It happened pretty fast. Since the minute I walked into her dance class I haven't been able to stop thinking about her. Have you seen her?"

She pointed to the front of the house.

He tracked her to Raven's favorite hiding spot in the small rock garden. "You trying to ditch me? Or are you just getting ready to run, now that I've subjected you to the White Feather gang?"

"Don't be like that, Jon. Everyone in your family has been great. But as I've been sitting here, trying to put a lid on all the doubts, and focus on these lovely clematis vines, I realized Jared does have a point—several of them in fact."

"Maggie—"

"Please don't deny it. There's stuff going on in your life you haven't talked about, so you have no right to get pissy with me."

"I wasn't pissy. Just surprised, okay?"

"So why are we avoiding a discussion about what happens next?"

Jon straddled the bench and gently grabbed her chin, forcing her to look at him. "We aren't avoiding it. We're prioritizing how we spend the time we do have together."

"Naked and sweaty?" she said with an edge.

"Something wrong with that? 'Cause, doll face, you sure didn't seem to mind last night. Or this morning."

Her eyes narrowed. "There's the *I-gave-it-to-you-good, baby*, rock-star attitude."

"Don't do that. That's not me, Maggie, and you damn well know it."

"Then tell me why you went out of town last week."

Fuck. He couldn't.

Yes, you can. Trust her. Tell her you're working on a project and that's all she can know for now.

But that was a lie. He'd rather dodge the question than lie to her. And that sucked because he didn't have anyone besides his agent to talk to—and Marty wasn't unbiased when it came to a potential commission. Jon was adrift on so many levels and he just wanted to forget about all the decisions hanging in the balance when he was alone with her. "Can we talk about this later?"

Maggie frowned. "You aren't blowing this off, right? Because it is important."

"I know. But so is this." He cupped the back of her neck, bringing her sweet mouth closer to kiss the frown right off her luscious lips.

"Great. Like I didn't get enough of watching you swallow my sister's face last time I saw you two together," Billy said behind them. "Classy."

Maggie opened her eyes, locking her gaze to Jon's before she broke the kiss with a smile. "Here's a piece of advice: the next time you see Jon and me in a private moment? Walk away so you won't get your virginal sensibilities offended."

Jon heard Eden snicker.

Maggie didn't stand; she just crossed her arms over her chest. "What are you doing here anyway?"

"Jim invited us."

He should've kept his mouth shut, but Jon still hadn't come to terms with all the bullshit that'd gone down in Billy's office a few weeks back. "So you show up for a White Feather family gathering, but you couldn't be bothered to drive to the CAM-PLEX in Gillette to support your sister at the regional dance finals yesterday?"

Billy's gaze turned razor sharp. "What are you talking

about?"

"Jon," Maggie warned, "let it go."

But he didn't. "I'm talking about the dance competition that Maggie and Seth have been training for, for months? Why weren't you there?"

Billy's mouth fell open. "The contest or dance-off or whatever it's called…was yesterday?"

Shit. Maggie hadn't told him?

Eden looked between Billy and Maggie. "Well, it appears *someone* forgot to tell us. So maybe you oughta tell us what gives, Maggie?"

Maggie's chin came up. "I didn't tell you because I was already on edge about competing after so many years away from it. Knowing how Billy feels about my dancing…can you really blame me?"

Jon disagreed. She should've at least given her brother the option of attending. And Billy wore such a look of sorrow Jon almost felt sorry for him.

Eden took a step forward. "I love you, Maggie, but that's a load of crap. I understand that it seemed like Billy didn't support your dance aspirations in the past, but that was years ago. Now you're the one making assumptions about what level of support he's willing to offer you? How about if the two of you boneheads leave the past in the past? Oh. And here's a novel idea. Talk to each other. Don't continue to fall back into those big-brother-little-sister roles." She whirled around and poked Billy in the chest. "That goes for you too, mister, when it comes to relationship stuff. Maggie and Jon are together. Find a better way to deal with it than sarcasm."

"Yes, ma'am."

"And because you're both here, we're gonna deal with the fallout from this right now. Billy, my beloved. Tell Maggie what you're feeling."

At first, Billy looked like he'd call bullshit on Eden's demand, but he kept his focus on Maggie. "I would've liked the chance to be in the audience cheering you on because I've never seen you dance like that."

"Maggie?" Eden said. "It's your turn."

"I don't hold a grudge about that. You always supported me in math and science and technology because those were things you understood. Tendu, tutus and relevé—not so much."

"I'm a worrier, Maggie. Add to the fact I'm an engineer, and your older brother and I'm an epic anal worrier." He smiled sadly. "I've always thought you were like me, but you're not, are you?"

"On some things. You had a career and life-altering revelation at age thirty-two. And here I am, dealing with the same thing."

Jon had a pang of guilt. There was a lot of stuff he and

Maggie hadn't talked about and rather than taking the chance and opening up to her a few minutes ago, he'd distracted her. No wonder his relationships were short-lived and he suspected it wasn't entirely due to his on-the-road lifestyle.

"I'm not making the choices you would," Maggie continued. "That doesn't make either of us right or wrong, just different."

"So you don't want my support?" Billy asked tightly.

Maggie got to her feet and hugged him. "I absolutely want your support. But I want you to remember I'll either thrive or fail on my own. But neither of those outcomes is on your shoulders this time."

"Old habits are hard to break, little sis."

"I get that. But you can transfer all that bossiness and overprotectiveness to baby Buchanan." She smirked. "I'm off the hook for at least the next eighteen years."

Billy laughed. And he hugged her. "Fair enough."

Eden clapped her hands. "See how much better everything is when you talk it out and everyone gets along?" She nudged her husband. "Now you and Jon shake hands."

Billy said, "Don't push it."

Maggie and Eden laughed, but Jon knew Billy wasn't trying to be funny.

"You guys going back to the party?" Eden asked.

Jon stood and draped his arm over Maggie's shoulder.

"No, we're leaving. But have fun."

"I'll call you this week," Maggie said to her brother.

It wasn't until they were in Jon's car that he realized what Maggie hadn't said. "You didn't tell him that you and Seth won."

She shrugged. "He won't be able to attend the finals anyway so there's no reason to make him feel guilty. Besides, I talked to my sister Lacy yesterday and she's already volunteered to fly to Florida and represent the Buchanan family. I know Billy will be good with that."

They didn't talk much on the way back to Maggie's place. He knew she was preoccupied so he didn't push.

She invited him inside. After she'd poured them both a glass of iced tea, she asked the question he'd been dreading.

"So Jon… How long were you and Eden together?"

IT DIDN'T ESCAPE Maggie's notice that Jon froze.

"What makes you think we were anything besides friends?"

Maggie rolled her eyes. "Look in the mirror, rock star. No woman would turn down a chance to get naked with you. Plus, my brother doesn't like you, which tells me you were more than friends with the woman he loves."

When Jon remained quiet, Maggie blurted, "Holy hell, Jon.

Please tell me you aren't still in love with her."

"No. I never was in love with her. Sad commentary, but we used each other for sex and neither of us pretended it was anything else. Then Billy came along, and after one night where the three of us got wild together, I saw how much Billy loved her, so I stepped out of the picture completely."

Maggie's mouth dropped open. "You had sex with my brother?"

"No. Jesus. I don't swing that way. You've been in bed with me, doll face, and you know how much I love pussy, so why would you even ask me that?"

"Because you're accepting of Jared and Gabe's relationship."

Jon frowned. "Jared isn't gay. He and Gabe are just roommates."

Evidently Jon had blinders on when it came to his little brother's sexual orientation and it wasn't her place to remove them. "My mistake. So what happened the night you three got wild?"

"Billy and I both had sex with Eden. Separately and together."

Silence. Then Maggie laughed. "I never thought my uptight brother had it in him to be a sexual wild man, let alone participate in a kinky threesome. But it makes sense why he didn't want you and me to get involved. 'Cause I'm pretty sure that wasn't your first or your last ménage."

"Nope." Jon kept his gaze on hers. "Now that you've heard my dark sexual secrets, you gonna hold stuff against me that happened a long time ago?"

She shook her head.

That seemed to surprise him. "Any wild nights you wanna share with me?" he asked lightly.

"My life—sex and otherwise—has been very tame compared to yours."

He flashed her that pure bad-boy grin. "Lucky thing you have me here to further your raunchy education."

Maggie raised an eyebrow. "The student becoming the teacher? Bring it."

"Well, I have had this fantasy of smacking your ass with a ruler."

"Not a chance, little drummer boy. But if you do well on the oral exam I might let you bang my erasers."

Twelve

THE NEXT WEEKEND was a blur of dancing, airports, trying to catch sleep, and discussion about routines and strategy. Maggie returned to Spearfish late Sunday night. Although exhausted, she called Jon and he insisted on coming over. Apparently he'd missed her as much as she'd missed him.

He'd be missing her a lot in the next eight weeks because Vladimir had agreed to coach them. She and Seth would be spending Friday, Saturday and half of Sunday in Salt Lake City.

While Maggie was pumped for the opportunity, she realized her life would not be her own for the next two months. They'd still need to rehearse the other four nights of the week, which meant driving back and forth every day. Although her hours at the doctor's office were somewhat flexible, she couldn't afford to take off every Friday from work and stay overnight in Rapid.

After scoring one of the best teachers in the business, there was no way Maggie could back out and take the job offer from the company in Billings. They required an immediate start date, not two months down the road after nationals, so she declined their offer.

Maggie heard a voice in the back of her head, calling her a fool for letting such a great job opportunity pass her by. At first she believed the voice belonged to her brother, but the louder it became, the more she realized it was her own.

Leaving the computer securities business hadn't been her choice. It'd been a blessing in disguise, giving her a break to evaluate her career and her life.

And now Jon was in her life. For how long?

Hopefully forever. If they could just get through the next few weeks with her hectic schedule they could sit down and figure out what to do for the long haul.

They'd just have to make it work.

THIS WASN'T WORKING.

Jon watched Maggie sleeping. They'd tumbled straight into bed after her late arrival from the airport. Even after three months together, sex between them continued to shake the rafters, but they rarely talked afterward anymore.

It'd been years since he'd forged a friends and lovers connection with a woman. Now that he had that, he missed that side of his relationship with Maggie. Just hanging out at his place or hers, doing their own things, but together. Indulging in normal couple stuff he'd neither had the time nor the interest in doing before.

So lately, when they had the rare chance to spend time together, Maggie was so tired or uptight all she wanted to do was sleep or fuck.

That would've suited Johnny Feather perfectly. But it didn't suit Jon White Feather at all.

It'd be hypocritical if he mentioned he was tired of only seeing her twice a week. Maggie was finally getting to live her dream—who was he to make any demands on her?

Besides, eight weeks of travel on weekends was a drop in the bucket, time wise, compared to how long he'd be gone if he took the tour spot with Push. Would she be all right with him being on the road for several months after he'd sworn he was taking a break from that lifestyle?

That's probably why he hadn't given them a solid answer— he wasn't sure if he was ready to go back to that untethered life when he might've finally found an anchor.

Jon was in limbo all the way around and he hated every second of it.

ONE GOOD THING about losing her job: Maggie had the

chance to teach, sharing both her love of dance and her love of technology. Teaching computer literacy to senior citizens in the afternoons twice a week took some of the sting out of her missing her spunky grandma, especially since a few of her students were from her grandmother's former nursing home.

Her teaching hour was up and she shelved the various laminated hint sheets in large type. She heard *squeak squeak* and saw her late grandmother's best friend wheeling toward her.

Hilda Helfenstein had the grandmother stereotype down cold: white hair, pleasantly plump, wearing a sweet smile, dowdy clothes and orthopedic shoes. However, behind her glasses were the shrewd eyes of a woman who'd seen a lot at age ninety-two. Her hearing might be spotty, and she had difficulty walking, but there wasn't anything wrong with her mind.

"Well, Maggie, you done good today. Even Ester followed along before she fell asleep."

"What about you? Did you find that link I told you about?"

Hilda sighed. "No. I accidentally forgot to type in the letter 'l' in *clock* and… Whoo-ee. Some of them pictures that popped up were…"

Maggie shuddered to think of the types of sites Hilda had stumbled across. "There should've been a security lock to block out those graphic images. I'll have the software fixed—"

"Don't you dare." Hilda gestured to the young woman from the rest home, who ran herd on the sometimes rowdy senior set. "Young Tiffany here was more embarrassed than me and kept trying to get me to leave the site, but I figured I was already there so I might as well look around." She shrugged. "I found out them young fellas ain't got nothin' on old Boris."

"Who is Boris?"

"The guy who lives in room one ten at the home. And he's got a solid ten inches, if you know what I mean."

How in the world had Hilda seen Boris's...? Maggie changed the subject. "What's on your agenda tonight?"

"Bingo, I think. What about you?" Hilda's birdlike gaze pinned her in place. "You need to get prettied up and go out and hook yourself a man."

"I already have a man."

"Is he good lookin'?" Hilda demanded.

"Very."

"Why haven't I met him?"

"Because I've been traveling a lot." That had become a point of contention between her and Jon and they'd exchanged a few harsh words about it two nights ago. So despite the fact she missed him, she'd suggested they needed time to cool off and he'd agreed.

"Bring him in sometime, dearie. So I can check him out.

Your granny would expect nothing less of me." She sighed. "I miss that wise woman."

"Me too."

Hilda backed away from the table and tossed over her shoulder, "Oh, you might take a look at that computer's cup holder. It's broken."

Cup holder? Maggie glanced at Tiffany, still lingering by the desk. "What is she talking about?"

"Hilda thought the CD drive was a cup holder. She pushed the button and complained that her coffee cup kept falling through."

Good lord. "Thanks for the heads up. I'll put in a request for Phil in repair to check it out."

Maggie had time to kill before she had to drive to Rapid City. Since the library wasn't busy, she settled in a comfy loveseat in the corner, propping her feet on the ottoman to catch up on gossip in the world of entertainment.

She'd finished *US Weekly* and *OK*, when she heard, "You know those rags are full of half truths and cleverly disguised lies, right?"

That voice was as smooth and warm as a snifter of brandy. Maggie glanced up into Jon's amused eyes. "Are you sure the actors on *Lost* aren't being stalked by a real-life smoke monster? Or that Zac Efron scored a recording contract only because he knocked up his *High School Musical* costar and they need the money for a gold-plated crib?"

Laughing, Jon plucked the *National Enquirer* from her hands. "I never would've guessed this was your choice for reading materials."

"What did you think I'd read?"

"A computer magazine. Or a book about dance techniques that will give you the edge to win the competition. Then you wouldn't have to be gone all the damn time."

She ignored his snarky comment and inhaled the musky aroma of his body-heat-warmed cologne. "I am multi-dimensional. I also read erotic romance."

He raised an eyebrow. "Is that where you learned the twisty move with your tongue? Because I really love that one." His voice dropped to a sexy growl. "Maybe we oughta sneak back to one of the study rooms. You can drop to your knees and give me another demonstration."

"In your dreams."

He slid next to her on the couch and stole a kiss. "I missed you."

"You must have if you tracked me down at the library."

"I got bored sitting at home. So anything exciting happen today, dancing queen?"

Casually, she said, "I got offered a job."

"With who?"

"A computer security company out of Fort Collins."

Jon gave her a sharp look. "When have you had time to interview with them?"

"Via phone and webcam. They sent me some encryption problems. Basic tech stuff tests."

"And you forgot to tell me?"

Why was he bristling? "Like you've told me about your last sudden and mysterious trip out of town?"

"Even if I would've wanted to talk to you about it, you haven't been around." He closed his eyes and took a deep breath. "Sorry. It's just I can't…never mind. This isn't about me. What did you say to the Fort Collins company?"

"I haven't given them an answer yet because I'm already committed to competing in nationals." She tipped her head back and stared at the yellowed acoustic ceiling tiles. "Accepting their offer should be a no brainer. A job in my field doesn't come along every day, especially not one where I can tele-commute from rural South Dakota. But if I took the job I'd have to give up dance. Then I'd be back to the same grind I was happy to leave. Yet, I could lead a somewhat normal life again."

"Is that what makes you want to take the job, Maggie? The chance to lead a normal life?"

Wait a second. Had Jon said that with some disdain? Probably not. Probably she was just imagining things. "That's part of it. The money is excellent. There are great benefits. Computer security is something I'm good at."

"You're good at dance," he countered.

"Obviously that's up in the air at this point. So the question is, do I take a sure thing—a steady job which will allow me to live around my friends and family"—*and you*—"hoping this company will hold the position for me for another month? Or do I chase a dream and remain in the same broke-ass position I'm in now? Which will be the bigger regret? If I don't take a chance? Or if I do?"

No response.

Maggie wasn't really asking for his advice as much as thinking out loud. Yes, she loved dancing, but she'd realized she wouldn't be totally fulfilled making it her career. Now that she had distance and perspective, wasn't that part of the reason she'd stopped dancing all those years ago? She knew she wasn't good enough to make a living doing it? She'd never blamed Billy for crushing her dream. She was stubborn enough that if she believed her brother had been blowing smoke, she wouldn't have fallen in line with his way of thinking. She would've stuck it out if only to prove him wrong.

Since clearing the air after regionals, Billy was the one person she could talk honestly to about her career issues. It'd shocked her when the companies she'd sent resumes to months ago, right after she'd lost her job, were now contacting her. She'd never believed the "we're keeping your resume on file" response, but apparently some companies really did that. A few months later those companies had openings and they were looking to her to fill them.

She glanced over at Jon, engrossed in *The National Enquirer*.

Glad my career crisis isn't as interesting as J-Lo's latest crash diet.

Not that she'd say anything to him—they were both a little testy in recent weeks and he never said anything about his career plans, so she let it slide.

Jon had set the biweekly music magazine *Tempest* on the ottoman and she picked it up, absentmindedly flipping through the pages. Toward the end in the "Deals and Steals" section, she stopped to tear out one of those annoying subscription cards, when she saw Jon's name—or rather, Johnny Feather's name. Included in the article were two pictures of him with the members of some band. She skimmed the paragraph below the photos:

Rumors are flying that Johnny Feather has flown the coop from the critically acclaimed Native American rock band Sapa. The drummer has recently been spotted in Seattle with Push and in L.A. with Darkly Dreaming, and Nashville with Radioactive Tar. He has reportedly auditioned for all three bands with an eye on touring with one of the groups this fall and is in final contract negotiations. The Whiskey A-Go-Go reportedly has Push scheduled to play next month. When contacted, representatives for the bands and the Indian rocker refused to comment.

So that's what Jon—no, Johnny Feather—had been doing? Maggie had stupidly believed him when he said he'd wanted to slow down and settle down, here, in Spearfish.

But he'd never said he'd be out of the public eye permanently.

Now that she thought about it, Jon had complained the last month about her flying to Salt Lake City every weekend, but he'd been evasive when speaking of his weekend plans. It'd made her feel guilty, thinking about him being home alone, when in actuality he'd been flying across the country auditioning for new bands? The thought he'd lied to her slashed her heartstrings; after three months together, she'd started to believe she was in love with him. Not that they'd made any promises to each other or spoken of a shared future, but Jon had implied it, plenty of times.

Hadn't he?

Or maybe she'd misunderstood.

Or maybe he'd just flat out lied to her.

Only one way to find out.

Maggie tossed the magazine in his lap and stood. "So I'm the last to know?"

Jon frowned. "Know what?"

She tapped on the article. "That you've got three prime drumming gigs dangling in front of you and you'll be on tour soon?"

He read the article before meeting her gaze. "No comment usually means the information is wrong."

"That isn't what I asked you."

"What do you want me to tell you?"

"The truth."

When he remained mum, she tossed out the first wild theory that popped into her head, hoping he'd scoff, deny it, or call her crazy.

"Here's what I think. You used the break from Sapa to tell everyone you wanted to take it easy for a while, when in reality, you were shopping yourself into a higher-profile band. You never had any intention of settling down, did you?"

Jon said nothing; he just leveled that implacable stare on her.

A sick feeling bloomed in the pit of her stomach. "When did you plan to tell me? Before I left for nationals? 'Oh, by the way, Maggie. I can't make it to watch you compete that weekend because I'll be in L.A. playing with Push. Oh, and I won't be here when you get back, I'll be on tour with Darkly Dreaming. Or Radioactive Tar. It's been fun. Have a nice life.'"

His mouth flattened into a thin line. "I wouldn't do that to you."

"Is that why you've encouraged me to keep dancing? Knowing I'd be traveling all the damn time, just like you will be? So you wouldn't have to feel guilty about lying to me?"

"No, I encouraged you to keep dancing because I know how much you love it." Jon stood. "Really, Maggie? You think I lied to you? You're going to throw accusations at me based on some bullshit article in a third-rate music magazine?"

"No. I'm asking you outright. Face to face. Is any of it true?"

"Yes, some of it is. But there are a lot of factors up in the air right now that I can't—"

"Stop. Just…stop." Maggie backed away. Mad. Frustrated. Confused. She looked at him and felt she didn't know him at all.

"Everything I said to you is true," Jon said evenly. "I want something permanent. Something stable. Something we've started to build. But it's not like we can talk about any of this when you're so focused on winning a national championship."

Talk about a smackdown. "You're right. It's all my fault. Even your secrets and your lies." She calmly picked up her satchel. "Good thing I don't have the time or the emotional energy to deal with anything else right now besides winning a national championship," she shot back. "And apparently I've been oblivious to a lot of things going on around me, so I apologize if you felt I was ignoring you and your career decisions. Oh right. You didn't even fucking *mention* it. So good luck with the band thing. I hope you win another fucking Grammy."

"Goddammit, Maggie, knock it off."

She slipped the strap over her shoulder and turned away.

He planted himself in front of her. "What are you doing?"

"Leaving for dance rehearsal."

"Sounds more like you're leaving me."

"I am." Before you can leave me.

"Like hell you are."

Don't cry. Stay mad. "Get out of my way."

"No, Maggie. Jesus. Wait. I didn't mean—"

"Leave me alone, Jon."

A librarian entered through the side stacks. "You two need to keep your voices down."

When Jon turned around to snarl at her, Maggie snuck out the back door.

And this time, he didn't bother to chase her down.

Probably for the best.

But she cried all the way to Rapid City anyway. More confused than she'd ever been. Her love life was up in the air. She might be facing two dead careers. She parked outside Seth's studio and stared at the door.

What was she supposed to do?

Her Grandma Ingrid's advice floated to the forefront, prophetic words after Maggie's first disastrous college dance class.

Take it one step at a time, girlie. You'll either find yourself dancing or walking the direction you need to go.

Taking a deep breath, Maggie knew that's all she could do. Take one step at a time. One day at a time.

Feet don't fail me now.

She got out of the car.

Thirteen

Orlando

Four weeks later…

JON COULDN'T BELIEVE it'd been a month since he'd seen Maggie. His heart ached even as it'd soared as he watched Maggie take the dance floor on Seth's arm. She looked beautiful, regal and confident—exactly the way he'd remembered her.

His stomach roiled with nervousness when the music started. He'd bought a seat close enough to the action to get a good look at her, but not in a conspicuous place she might see him—because this wasn't about him, or them, but her living her dream.

So it was hard as hell to sit on his hands when the semi-finalists names were called and Maggie and Seth hadn't made it past the first round.

Jon stayed through the semi-finals, lingering in the empty

arena after the spectators and the competitors had left, knowing Maggie would eventually wander out. The cleaning crew was done sweeping up popcorn and the set-up crew was preparing for the next event. It took every ounce of patience to wait for her to come to him, instead of tracking her down.

Much had happened in the last month. He'd made a lot of professional decisions and faced a lot of personal demons. Jon just hoped he wasn't too late to explain those changes to Maggie.

He heard the *click click* of her shoes first, echoing to him like a drumbeat. She emerged from the tunnel leading backstage and she looked so damn good his heart nearly stopped. She'd changed out of her sparkly costume and into street clothes. Hair scraped into a ponytail. Her ever-present duffel bag hung over her shoulder. But a sort of sadness surrounded her that he could see from up in the stands.

She strolled around the edges of the arena floor. Tipping her head back to look at the lights, the sound system and the huge TV screens that were now dark.

Was she lamenting it'd just been the luck of the draw that she and Seth had been entered in the same flight as the reigning champions? Probably Maggie would take that as some sort of sign. He'd never known anyone who could be called a romantic pragmatist, but she certainly fit the bill.

No one could say she and Seth hadn't given their all to

their performance. They'd danced well. Better than they had at regionals. But the other couples in the competition had been better.

How did that make her feel? Had the competition stirred up her competitive streak? Would she be determined to work harder? Or would she back off and reevaluate whether she wanted to pursue getting to the next level in the world of competitive dancing?

Stop lurking and go find out.

Jon waited until Maggie sat on the player's bench before leaving the shadows. She was so lost in thought she didn't hear his approach until he sat next to her. "Hey."

Maggie gasped softly. "Jon? Oh my God. What are you doing here?"

"I came to watch you compete."

She blinked at him as if he were an apparition. "Why?"

"You know why," he said softly, keeping his gaze locked on hers. "I remembered the night after you won regionals you said you liked walking around a venue after it ended to see if any crowd energy lingered."

"I'm surprised you remembered that."

"I remember a lot of things about you, Maggie. Everything in fact."

She glanced down to where her fingers were twisting the straps of her duffel bag. "So you saw us dance?"

"Yes. You guys were good."

"But not good enough."

Typical Maggie response in that no bitterness laced her tone.

"So are you okay?"

"Yes. No. I don't know." She sighed heavily. "Honestly? It all seems pretty surreal. The hours spent rehearsing. The anticipation of getting to wear a gorgeous costume and dancing in front of thousands of people. The fear of failing in front of thousands of people. What a rush."

"It is a serious rush. But it always wears off."

"You would know."

Jon drummed his fingers on the bench beside him, at a loss for what to say.

"And now that we've exchanged polite small talk…maybe you should tell me why you're really here."

"Because even though things were left at a standstill between us, I knew it was temporary and I gave you the space you needed. But I didn't stop thinking about you. Or caring about you. This competition is a big deal in your life and I wanted to be here to support you."

Maggie looked at him. "Wasn't this the weekend you were supposed to play a live show with Push?"

He shrugged. "I told them I had a prior commitment."

"And they didn't mind you bailing on them?" she asked

skeptically.

Don't bristle. He kept his tone light. "Hadn't you heard all musicians are flaky like that?"

"Not you. I'd never lump you in with all musicians, Jon."

"But you did."

She was quiet for a moment. "I guess I did. Why is it hard for me to take a leap of faith and so damn easy to jump to conclusions?"

"Human nature. People make mistakes. I did. I should've told you what was going on."

"So what is going on?"

"Push's management got a little pissy about me changing my mind and I realized I don't wanna work with people like that."

"When did you back out of the gig?"

"Last month."

"But…" Her eyes searched his and she seemed totally bewildered.

He knew the feeling. "Yes, that was before I knew whether we'd work this out. I wasn't ready to walk away from you then and that hasn't changed." Jon forced himself to slow down. "I had no idea the music trade mags were snapping pictures and causing all kinds of trouble."

Maggie lifted a brow.

"Look, I'm not blaming the paparazzi for how you found

out. I could give you a bullshit answer like I'd signed a bunch of nondisclosure agreements—which is true—but the truth is I'm so used to dealing with all this business crap myself, I haven't learned to open up to anyone. I should've trusted you and talked to you about it. I didn't. I'm sorry. It'll never happen again, I promise."

"So are you going back on tour?"

"No. I really am taking time off indefinitely. The offers were tempting, hell they were flattering which was probably why I even considered them. But I've honestly never been happier, just working on my own stuff on my own time frame, and learning to have a life. I want a life with you, Maggie." He tapped his fingers on his knees. "Sorry. Here I am babbling on—"

She put her hand over his. "You're doing that drumming thing. Why are you nervous?"

"Because I have so many things I want to say, but I wasn't sure if you'd tell me to shove off before I'd get to tell you a single one."

"Ironically enough, I have a lot of things to say to you too." Then she leaned forward to kiss him. "But I planned on sucking back a few cosmos to get up the courage before I drunk dialed you."

He laughed softly and the fear inside him settled a little. "Do you have any idea how crazy I am about you?"

"I've got a pretty good idea since you're here and since I feel the same way."

"God, I missed you."

"I missed you too."

Jon framed her face in his hands. "I don't want to fuck this up again, Maggie."

"Me either, but you don't get to take all the blame for it, Jon. It was a mutual fuck up. But that means we get to start from scratch." She turned her head and kissed the inside of his wrist. "You game for that, rock star?"

"Absolutely."

They didn't speak for several moments. Then Maggie sighed. "I have a confession to make. I took the job with the security company from Fort Collins."

That surprised him. "When?"

"A month ago."

"But that was before…"

"I competed in nationals? Yep. I knew going into this it would be my one shot at a championship. I'm disappointed we didn't win, but I am excited to start my new job."

He was excited too, if it meant what he thought it did. "This is the telecommuting one, right? You'll be living in Spearfish?"

"Yes. I will have to travel to Fort Collins periodically, but I can deal with that. Can you?"

"Heck yeah, maybe we'll turn it into a road trip." Jon's

thumb stroked her cheek. "Because I never want to be away from you for very long."

Maggie kissed him again. "Same here. I'm happy I reconnected with my love of dancing because it led me to you. But I also finally understand dancing will only ever be a hobby for me. I'm good with that. And Seth understands. In fact, he's turned over all the upcoming dance classes at the community center to me."

Jon's eyes lit up. "So does that mean you'll be looking for a new permanent dance partner?"

"Uh-huh, but it ain't gonna be you, because sweetheart, you suck."

He nudged her shoulder. "I'm blaming you for that."

Her nose wrinkled. "Why's that?"

"Because you still owe me a dance lesson."

"You think one dance lesson will bring you up to snuff, rock star?"

"Hell no." He kissed her softly. Thoroughly. With such a burst of happiness, he felt like doing a jig. And wouldn't that make her laugh?

"Your seductive kisses won't change the fact it's gonna take me forever to teach you how to dance. You know that, right?"

"Yep. That's what I'm hoping for. A lifetime of dance lessons."

Also by
LORELEI JAMES

Rough Riders Legacy Series

UNBREAK MY HEART

Rough Riders Series

LONG HARD RIDE
RODE HARD
COWGIRL UP AND RIDE
TIED UP, TIED DOWN
ROUGH, RAW AND READY
BRANDED AS TROUBLE
STRONG, SILENT TYPE (NOVELLA)
SHOULDA BEEN A COWBOY
ALL JACKED UP
RAISING KANE
SLOW RIDE (short story)
COWGIRLS DON'T CRY
CHASIN' EIGHT
COWBOY CASANOVA
KISSIN' TELL
GONE COUNTRY
SHORT RIDES (NOVELLA ANTHOLOGY)
REDNECK ROMEO
COWBOY TAKE ME AWAY
LONG TIME GONE (novella)

Need You Series

WHAT YOU NEED
JUST WHAT I NEEDED
ALL YOU NEED
WHEN I NEED YOU

Blacktop Cowboys® Series

CORRALLED
SADDLED AND SPURRED
WRANGLED AND TANGLED
ONE NIGHT RODEO
TURN AND BURN
HILLBILLY ROCKSTAR
ROPED IN (novella)
STRIPPED DOWN (novella)
WRAPPED AND STRAPPED
STRUNG UP (novella)
HANG TOUGH
TRIPPED OUT (novella)

Mastered Series

BOUND
UNWOUND
SCHOOLED (digital only novella)
UNRAVELED
CAGED

Wild West Boys Series

MISTRESS CHRISTMAS
MISS FIRECRACKER

Single Title Novellas

LOST IN YOU (short novella)
WICKED GARDEN
DIRTY DEEDS

CPSIA information can be obtained
at www.ICGtesting.com
Printed in the USA
LVHW04s2028020718
582512LV00001B/36/P